THE CALLING BIRDS

THE FOURTH DAY

JACQUI NELSON

Cover design by Erin Dameron-Hill

ISBN ebook: 978-0-9958596-3-0
ISBN print: 978-0-9958596-2-3

For my mom, Mary Nelson,
who raised me to love not only flowers but
every marvel on earth, including birds and mules
and, of course, horses and books.

CHAPTER 1

Christmas Eve
December 24, 1876

*B*irdie Bell scanned the inside of Noelle's Golden Nugget Saloon searching for a man she'd never met but had agreed to marry in order to escape every lawman, outlaw, and fortune hunter in Colorado and beyond. She'd once again made a mess of her life, this time in an unprecedented string of impulsive decisions.

She shouldn't have opened her dress shop in Denver and bought all of those gorgeous fabrics. She shouldn't have ducked into Mrs. Walters' Benevolent Society of Lost Lambs after she'd glimpsed the legendary fugitive hunter, Lachlan Bravery, and his wife, Yellow Feather, on the street. She shouldn't have expressed a desire to not only relocate towns but change her life.

But most of all, she should not have agreed to Mrs. Walters' suggestion that if Birdie wished to marry, then the matchmaker knew a man who ran a freighting business and who needed a wife. Jack Peregrine could easily arrange to transport Birdie's treasure trove of fabrics and partially made dresses to his home in the remote town of Noelle.

Genevieve Walters' raised voice filled the saloon as she continued to berate the town's reverend. Noelle was not the place he'd assured the woman it would be. Birdie wasn't surprised. Her family had moved to a mining town when she was fifteen. Every town was the same but different—always disappointing but usually when you least expected it.

Still, Noelle had already delivered one much-appreciated gift.

Despite a grueling journey up a mountain in a snowstorm—that had only been possible in wagons specially fitted with sleigh runners, Birdie's possessions had arrived safely in Noelle. As had she and the eleven other brides under Mrs. Walters' care.

The matchmaker wanted to save the women. The men wanted to save their town.

Not for the first time, Birdie questioned her wants. Had she really agreed to come here and marry a man she knew only from a few letters? Just to hold onto a wagonload of cloth sitting outside the saloon?

She was trading one form of bondage for another. Freedom only came from a willingness to leave every place she'd ever lived in a heartbeat. Drop everything. Run with only the clothes on her back and two essentials: her father's compass on a chain beneath her bodice and her mother's scissors on the sewing chatelaine around her waist. As long as she could chart a fast course with her compass and mend her life later with her sewing—which had always paid for food and shelter—she could outrun her past and start over.

And over. And over.

She stifled a sigh. No freedom there either. Would she

ever break the cycle? Fourteen years had passed. Lives had ended. Memories had faded. Unfortunately, a lost shipment of stolen gold was hard to forget.

If anyone discovered her real identity, she'd lose not only her liberty but possibly her life. The law would lock her up and demand she tell them where her brothers had hidden their last heist. Others would just press a knife to her throat or a gun to her head and take a more direct path in their questioning.

It had happened before.

Luckily her small size, her scissors, and once even a needle had helped her escape until she got savvy enough to never be captured again.

Mrs. Walters clutched a stack of letters she'd pulled from her bag and continued to rail at Reverend Hammond. "You described the pristine buildings, homey atmosphere and well-appointed rooms where we would be able to rest before the weddings!"

A wedding might lead to a family. The thought kept resurrecting memories.

I miss you, Maman et Papa, and our lives in Montreal. Before the Cariboo Gold Rush lured them west and destroyed everything. She exhaled a slow breath, hoping to expel her resentment. It was exhausting carrying around this much anger for dead men and their deeds.

She should've been able to shout to the heavens that she was proud to be Bernadette Bellamy and the sister of two admirable brothers. *I miss you as well, mes frères, even though you fell so low. You ruined so much more than your lives and mine.*

She wouldn't repeat their mistakes. She'd only lead a life where hard work built a person's fortune. She was not a thief.

Mrs. Walters addressed the brides now. Birdie stood on the edge of their group, trying to listen while she continued watching the men.

Mayor Hardt had departed after wringing the reverend's neck and calling him a backstabbing skunk for writing letters on his behalf to the bride named Felicity Partridge. Felicity was no stranger to creating disturbances. In Denver, Birdie had heard rumors that the woman had been arrested for leading a women's rights rally.

Silas, the groom who'd claimed the mayor had written his letters to his intended, Penny Jackson, was still belly-aching about his tooth. It'd broke when the arguing men bumped into Penny who'd then had the bad luck to stumble against her betrothed as he took a drink of whiskey. *Et alors! The poor woman was unlucky.*

Would her luck be any better? Her husband-to-be hadn't made himself known, and no one had mentioned his name. However, in a town as small as this, most of the men probably knew him.

She could ask one to point out Mr. Peregrine. She could but she wouldn't. A person often learned more by watching and waiting for revelations.

A man with a limp approached Reverend Hammond.

Her interest perked. The businessman she'd promised to marry had written that he'd lost his leg in the war. This man also had a badly scarred face and only one eye. Her groom hadn't mentioned those injuries. Her gaze moved to the bar. Maybe Mr. Peregrine was there.

The reverend's voice was nearly too low to hear, but his words chilled her blood. "Sheriff, I have a job for you, and it isn't going to be pleasant."

Disbelief then fear clenched her heart. This town had a lawman? What was the unpleasant job? Was it her?

She spun toward the door and froze. Too many people stood in her way. She'd create a spectacle running through them. From the corner of her eye, she studied the sheriff. How had she missed the man's deadly looking revolvers and expression to match?

She strained to hear what the reverend was telling him. She only caught bits. "Mayor Hardt...owns the lease on *La Maison des Chats*...get his permission to have the girls moved."

The lawman nodded, said something she couldn't decipher, and left the saloon.

Her heart started beating properly again. She was still safe. But for how long?

Slowly, so as not to draw attention, she threaded her way through the throng. She only stopped when she stood with her back against the wall by the door. Ready to race out and disappear in the blizzard if need be.

When Mrs. Walters announced that their accommodations were ready, Birdie was out the door first. She made a beeline for the wagons. She'd ask the driver of the one carrying her bundles of fabrics to follow her wherever Mrs. Walters was now taking them.

The street was empty. Only the grooves made by the sleigh runners remained in the snow, and not for long. The storm was quickly filling them. The rig carrying everything she owned had vanished.

Panic ripped the air from her lungs. She spun in a circle, searching. She nearly cried out when the driver trudged out of a snow flurry. He halted by the saloon door, waiting for the brides to file out so he could go in.

She jumped in front of him. "Where's your wagon?"

He yelped in surprise, then laughed. "You startled me,

miss. Your group appears to be leaving without you. You might want to—"

"No." She crossed her arms. "I'm not going anywhere. Not until you tell me what you've done with my belongings."

He gulped and said in a rush, "I couldn't leave the mules standing in a snowstorm. So, I took 'em to Mr. Burnside's barn. I dropped your baggage inside Peregrines' Post and Freight before I did." He gestured in the direction he'd come. The opposite way that Mrs. Walters was headed with the brides.

"That won't do. It won't do at all. My inventory must stay with me."

The man rubbed the back of his neck and frowned at the snow falling around them. He'd done his job and got them to town. She couldn't ask him to do more.

But she also couldn't stop herself from asking, "How safe is the freight office? Are there many thefts in Noelle?"

He shook his head vigorously. "Not since Sheriff Draven came to town."

Her stomach plummeted to her boots. Noelle's lawman was the fearsome bounty hunter, Draven? She'd never have come to Noelle if she'd known he was here. The minute she'd heard the stories about Draven, she'd added his name to the top of the list of men she never wanted to meet. Had he retired from the hunt? It didn't matter. He was now a sheriff, and she had a history with a band of notorious outlaws.

But he hadn't recognized her, and why should he? As long as her real name remained secret, she was safe. Draven's presence in town might help keep her treasures safe, as well. But even that formidable man couldn't control the weather.

She observed the wagon driver closely. "What about

leaks and drafts?" She didn't want her fabrics getting wet. "How sturdy is the office's construction?"

"It's top notch. Mr. Peregrine built it and he doesn't do things half-measure."

"Why didn't he—?"

"Don't dawdle, Birdie." Mrs. Walters cut her off before she could finally ask why her groom hadn't come to meet her. "Stay close to me and the ladies."

The driver seized his opportunity and fled into the saloon.

"We need to get out of this snow," Mrs. Walters added, "and into our accommodations."

Birdie gazed longingly in the opposite direction that the reverend was leading the brides. She had no idea where he was taking them. Mrs. Walters probably didn't either. It might be as bad as the saloon.

The reverend's words came back to her. *La Maison des Chats*. The House of Cats. A house of prostitution.

The driver's description of the freight office as "top notch" sounded much better. She'd have to trust that her belongings would be safer away from her than with her —for now.

She fell into step with the brides and raised the hood of her long coat when the wind whipped the snow in their faces. The sting didn't stop her from scanning her surroundings. Not that there was much to see. The women trudged through a world shrouded in white.

Even at seventy-five years of age, Agatha Boonesbury's spunky nature and youthful agility kept her at the front of the pack where she hovered close to Kezia Mirga, the gypsy widow. Kezia's tall stature put her a head above the other brides. Her vibrant purple cloak edged in embroidered gold thread made her stand out even more while at the same time it concealed the bundle of her darling baby daughter.

Molly Norris' not-so-darling goose kept wiggling out of his owner's embrace and biting anyone who came too close. The brides had learned the hard way to give Molly's protective pet as wide a berth as possible. Free of the close confines of the wagons, most of the women continued clumping together, forming friendships as well as sharing their body heat.

On the journey up the mountain, Birdie had handed out her warmest fabric to some who hadn't anything more than a shawl. Still, the women shivered. Not for the first time, guilt pricked her for being snug inside her coat while others suffered.

She'd painstakingly tailored the garment to fit her size and needs exactly. She wore the finest wool cut the perfect length to shield her entire body but also allow for easy movement—including running.

Why hadn't her groom come running to meet her?

She'd read his letter so many times she'd committed the first paragraphs to memory.

Miss Bell, I have limitations you should be aware of before you agree to be my wife and come to Noelle. My life is not for the faint-hearted. I was married once. While the union was long, it was not fruitful. Nevertheless, I bear the weight of family commitments.

Hard work and hard choices must be accepted for our family business to prosper in Noelle even if I cannot. I lost my leg in a mule train freighting accident in the war. I am no longer a whole man.

Was her groom bedridden? The startling question made

her stumble and nearly fall in the snow. She'd written to him that she was thirty, but he hadn't shared his age. Why hadn't Mr. Peregrine been clearer?

Suddenly, she saw his letter for what it was: a warning written under duress. His conscience and the town were forcing his hand. Jack Peregrine needed a wife, but deep down he didn't believe Birdie should come to Noelle and marry him.

CHAPTER 2

*J*ack limped out of the Golden Nugget Saloon
and half-ran, half-hopped down the street. He
gritted his teeth against the jarring of his stump
against his wooden leg and the pull of the deepening drifts
slowing him down. He squinted through the pelting snow.
He couldn't see a solitary person. Where was Gus?

His grandfather's growing absentmindedness and bouts
of disorientation made wandering off in the winter distress-
ingly dangerous. What if he fell in the snow and froze to
death before Jack could find him?

Gus hadn't been inside the saloon or any of the busi-
nesses he'd stopped at after racing out of the freight office in
search of him. Half of the buildings had been empty.

He'd found out why in the saloon. The brides had
arrived. Could his luck get any worse? He'd lost Gus *again*
and he'd missed meeting his bride and his first chance to
make a good impression with her.

The men in the saloon had told him that the matchmaker, Mrs. Walters, had demanded that her brides be
housed in the best building in town. Reverend Hammond

had left mere minutes ago to escort them to *La Maison des Chats*, the town whorehouse.

Had everyone lost their minds?

As he rounded the corner and came in sight of *La Maison*, a grand two-story structure that was indeed the best construction in Noelle, he saw a thin man with red hair disappear inside the front door.

Hallelujah! He'd found Gus. Or at least he'd cornered him.

Running in the frigid air had burned his lungs raw by the time he reached *La Maison* and slipped inside. A crowd of women filled the front hall. One of them was his bride, Birdie Bell.

A hard-working woman who'd formed her own dress-making business in Denver. A mature woman of thirty. A strong woman who wouldn't break under life's hardships.

Maybe his luck would change today. With time Miss Bell might come to respect or even enjoy his company. He needed this marriage to last.

He should've looked for Gus first, but he couldn't stop scanning the women in search of his bride. Even windswept from the storm and huddled together shivering from the cold—or perhaps the knowledge that they stood in a house of ill repute—the women were a fine-looking bunch. How had Mrs. Walters managed that?

A raven-haired, pale-skinned woman standing slightly apart from the rest caught his attention. Her beauty would've been enough to hold any man spellbound but her tiny size made him rigid with concern.

A woman so small wouldn't last long in a town like Noelle.

His worry turned to anger. Whoever had asked her to come here should be horsewhipped!

A faint smile curved her mouth as if she was amused by the prospect of being housed in a brothel. He must be dreaming. She shouldn't be here and she couldn't be amused.

She surveyed the room, studying everything and everyone, until she saw him. Then she stared at him the way he felt he must be staring at her, as if mesmerized.

"I've come for a bride," a voice proclaimed loudly, a familiar voice that made him cringe. "Which one of you is the future Mrs. Peregrine?"

The woman spun to face the speaker—his Grandpa Gus.

A wave of gasps and tittering laughter swept the crowd. Several of the women glanced at the tiny woman who'd captivated him. She was now contemplating Gus with wide eyes.

Her gaze darted to him. When she found him still observing her, her expression went blank and devoid of emotion.

She squared her shoulders, strode straight up to Gus, and said in a lyrical voice with a seductively foreign accent, "I am the bride you seek, Mr. Peregrine. My name is Birdie Bell."

A surge of euphoria followed quickly by alarm made him stagger and lean heavily against the nearest wall. This tiny Frenchwoman couldn't be Miss Bell. He asked for a strong woman. This one wouldn't be able to hold up under his workload, the rough town, or the surrounding wilderness. She'd abandon Noelle and him.

Could he blame her if she did?

If she didn't, she might die here.

"No!" His voice shot out louder than Gus' a moment ago.

Complete silence descended around him. The chance to

make a good impression was long gone. Everyone in the front hall stared at him including his tiny bride.

He limped toward her.

Her gaze dropped to his leg and her lips parted on a gasp. When their eyes met again, she smiled. He'd told her in his letter that he'd lost a leg in the war. She'd guessed who he was.

Did the prospect of marrying him please her or was she merely relieved she wouldn't be marrying a man forty years older than her?

He realized he'd wrote that Peregrines' Post and Freight was a family run business but he'd been remiss in not describing the members of his family.

"Sorry for being late. I'm Jack Peregrine and this is my grandfather, Gus Peregrine. Will you—" He'd been about to ask if she'd come home with him and stay in his brother's, Max, empty room. It'd be better than residing in a whore-house, but it probably wouldn't be appropriate for them to live together before they were married.

He could ask her to say her vows with him right now and then—

What if she said no? What if she said yes?

Her smile faded to a shadow of its former brilliance. She raised her chin and studied him with eyes dark as blue twilight and glittering with questions. She'd soon see that they weren't the right match. But he needed a wife.

He needed to reassess his plans.

"I'll call on you tomorrow, Miss Bell. I must take my grandfather home." He grabbed Gus by the elbow and pulled him away.

His bride's gaze stayed on him until he crossed *La Maison's* threshold and shut the door behind him.

CHAPTER 3

*a*fter sharing a meal in the whorehouse's ground floor kitchen with Mrs. Walters and the other brides, Birdie paused at the bottom of the stairs. Despite being bone tired, her chaotic thoughts made her too jittery to go upstairs and sleep.

She'd finally met her groom. The saloon had been packed with men. None of them had held her attention. Not even the fearsome sheriff.

Then a tawny-haired lion of a man had entered *La Maison*'s front hall. Her gaze went to the door, longing to see him again.

Why was he different? Many of the men in Noelle were not only tall and handsome but muscular from the strenuous trades associated with a mining town. But Jack Peregrine had watched her like she was the only person in the room. She'd regarded him the same way. She wanted him and only him.

When his grandfather had spoken, her hopes had been dashed, but quickly resurrected. She'd never been so happy to discover a man had a limp. But despite their interest in each other, Jack Peregrine walked away from her.

He'd left her in a whorehouse rather than take her home with him.

She probably shouldn't fault him overly for that. He had a befuddled relative to care for. Jack had exhibited a great deal of concern and care for his feisty grandfather. He'd apologized for being late meeting her. He'd said he'd call on her tomorrow.

He'd also shouted the word "no" immediately after she'd told his grandfather her name. That rejection still rang in her ears. Similar to Jack's letters, the first word from his mouth sounded like he didn't want her in Noelle.

He wasn't the only one.

Madame Bonheur had strenuously protested the removal of her working girls, and herself, to a building across the street. When the woman's argument with Mrs. Walters and the reverend erupted in the hall, Birdie had been upstairs with Felicity, Kezia, Agatha, and Maybelle—who from the moment she joined the brides hadn't stopped complaining about everyone while bragging endlessly about herself.

Pearl, the only soiled dove who'd stayed, had been helping them settle into their shared bedroom. The woman's welcoming manner and soothing voice had immediately put Birdie at ease. But her slender figure, honey-blonde hair, and pale blue eyes had made Birdie's imagination race with possibilities.

Pearl was a dressmaker's dream.

Birdie's hand fell from the staircase railing to tap the velvet sewing case attached to her chatelaine belt. If she had access to her fabrics, she'd already be creating a replacement for Pearl's dress. While not vulgar, the woman's clothing wasn't respectable either, nor was it anywhere good enough for such a kind but also protective soul.

Pearl had used her body to barricade their bedroom door rather than let the curious brides rush out for even a peek at the madam. At first, the gesture had puzzled Birdie. Then it had filled her with outrage.

What had Madame Bonheur done to Pearl to make the woman jump so swiftly to shield the brides from her employer?

Birdie's hand jumped as well—to her scissors hanging next to her sewing case. If she ever heard Madame's voice again, she'd be ready to defend herself.

The brothel owner's fake French accent would make her easily recognizable.

Even now the tone and the reason behind using it—the demand to appear more exotic and elicit men's carnal attention—made Birdie cringe. Thankfully her sewing skills had saved her from the life of a French whore.

Frenchmen had so many more opportunities. They also had their own challenges. Like being too proud and hot-tempered to bend under an English tyranny to the north. The Colony of British Columbia may have joined the Dominion of Canada since her time there, but she doubted if the change would've made any difference to her brothers.

Prejudices ran deep. She'd be foolish to hope it'd be any different in Noelle. She'd do well to find out more about this town and the people who ruled it.

Had Sheriff Draven heard about her brothers? Was he familiar with northern outlaws and robberies? Did he work alone? Did he answer to the mayor or the reverend? How friendly was he with Jack Peregrine?

She needed to question someone with intimate knowledge of the town.

Voices in a side room drew her attention. The reverend had pointed it out as a parlor. Inside, Pearl was once again helping several brides get comfortable.

When Minnie Gold saw Birdie standing in the doorway, the woman kindly beckoned for her to come in and join them. "Are you missing your sewing as much as I miss my embroidery?"

She felt her eyes widen in surprise. Minnie had spoken to her in perfect French—an unusual skill for a lady's maid. "Where did you learn to speak French so beautifully?" she asked.

Minnie ducked her head and replied in English, "I had a close relationship with my mistress. She taught me many things." Her voice grew hushed and hoarse. "We were like sisters."

Birdie found herself nodding and frowning at the same time. This might explain why the maid carried herself with the grace and manners of a highborn lady, but she couldn't help thinking that Minnie wasn't being completely honest with her or the others.

She continually modified her own words and actions, so she could perfect the art of concealing rather than revealing. She sensed that the women in this room were doing the same.

Cara Donnelly smiled easily and often, especially at the new fur hat, woolen coat and warm-looking boots she'd worn during their trip to Noelle. The flame-haired Irish-woman had come well prepared, but whenever she said her last name it came out with an undercurrent of tension or an edge of unfamiliarity.

Molly Norris perched on the edge of her seat, holding her goose close but also away from Cara and Minnie. Her long hair kept falling forward to partially conceal the scar that ran from her eye down her nose to her lip. The wound looked new. Possibly only a few weeks old. It might fade, but Molly would never be free of the mark or her obvious love for a bird that she treated like the dearest of friends.

Avis Smith sat in the corner, positioning herself—as had become her routine—slightly distant from everyone else. She adjusted her bonnet and gloves while she kept her dark-brown eyes fixed on the Bible that was her constant companion.

Like Birdie, these women had secrets they wished to hide.

She would've liked to get to know them better or at least offer them more comfort than the fabric she'd handed out during the journey up the mountain, but Pearl was the only local left in *La Maison* who could answer her questions.

She drew in a deep breath, pushed aside her concern and curiosity, and claimed the chair closest to Pearl. The prostitute gave her a welcoming smile as the chatter between Minnie, Cara, and Molly resumed.

She returned Pearl's smile but said nothing. Probably best to eavesdrop on the conversation in progress and see what it revealed. Unfortunately, the discussion kept circling around the fact they were being housed in a whorehouse and that when—or now more accurately *if* they got married, they'd say their vows in a saloon.

Even worse Pearl had gone silent.

She drummed her fingers on her sewing case. Without any fabric, she could do nothing with the needles and thread inside. Her hand moved to the pencil and miniature notepad also hanging from her belt.

She kept listening as she sketched a new dress design. A poor one. As usual, something was missing. She wouldn't know what until she started sewing. What was Jack doing?

Was he working? His letters had mentioned lots of work. She shook her head, added another line to her design, and tried to focus on the voices around her.

A hesitant hand touched her pencil. She realized she'd once again stopped drawing. She glanced up to find Pearl staring longingly at her tiny sketchpad.

"May I?" the woman asked.

No one else was in the parlor. When had they left? She quickly handed the pencil and paper to Pearl—to keep her from leaving as well and because the woman looked so keen to hold them.

"Have you lived in Noelle long?" she asked.

The pencil in Pearl's hand flew across the page with sure strokes. "Long enough."

"I heard that Noelle has a lawman named Sheriff Draven. Do you know him?"

Pearl went very still. Unnaturally still. Finally she said, "He's a frequent customer, yes."

Birdie silently berated herself for being insensitive. A lifetime of running away from people rather than staying with them had stunted her social skills. She hoped Pearl wouldn't run away from her. "Forgive me for asking. I'm worried about losing my inventory."

"What inventory?"

Birdie breathed a sigh of relief when Pearl began drawing again.

"I had a dress shop in Denver before coming to Noelle. I brought dozens of bundles of fabric and partially made dresses with me. I've started garments in all sorts of sizes in the hopes I'd find owners for them. They now reside in Peregrines' Post and Freight while I'm here unable to watch over them and keep them safe. Noelle is lucky to have a sheriff, but...does he work alone or have a deputy to help him?"

"He's all alone." An uncomfortable silence stretched between them, but at least Pearl didn't stop drawing this time. "I mean, the mayor pays him to protect the town, and I don't think he needs anyone's help."

The news increased Birdie's relief and her worry. She only had one lawman to watch out for, but he was still the worst one possible. Or had he mellowed lately?

"A sheriff's job must take him many places. Did an interest in mining bring Draven to Noelle?"

"Two years ago, he was wounded in a shoot-out with the Quigg gang and staggered into town." Pearl's voice had gone breathless as she recounted the event. "Doc Deane fixed him up and Mayor Hardt hired him." She stopped abruptly, shrugged and handed back Birdie's pencil and sketchpad. "That's all I know."

Pearl had not only completed Birdie's dress design but transformed it into a masterpiece. "*C'est incroyable*, Pearl! What a talent you have. *Dieu te bénisse!* Thank you for helping me and all of the brides."

Pearl smiled shyly. "Try to get some sleep. Tomorrow you'll be back with your sewing and your groom."

Birdie's shoulders slumped. "I hardly know the man."

"Who have you been paired with?"

"Jack Peregrine." Birdie bristled with an unfamiliar jealousy. Had Jack been Pearl's customer? She watched for a change in Pearl's demeanor as she asked, "Do you know him?"

"Don't worry." Pearl's posture assumed none of her earlier tension when they'd discussed Draven. "You and your inventory will be safe with Jack. He's as dedicated to his business as he is to his family."

The word *dedicated* drained the rigidity from her body. "I'm relieved to hear you say this. *Merci.*"

Pearl rose to leave. "But if you need the sheriff, look for him in his jail. He lives in the first building on the left as you head toward Peregrines' Post on the other side of town."

Bon Dieu! She'd have to walk by Draven's residence every day? No, twice a day. Every morning and night if she remained unmarried and unable to move in with her husband. That would be courting disaster.

She had to make a decision. Then she had to ensure that it happened. Tomorrow she was either getting married or she was loading her bundles of inventory into another wagon and leaving Noelle and Jack Peregrine.

CHAPTER 4

The 1st day of Christmas
December 25, 1876

"What the blazes happened here?" The door connecting Jack's carpentry shop to the back of the freight office slammed behind him with a bang that echoed his bellow of disbelief.

Bright rolls of fabric, heaps of ribbon, lace, and partially made dresses lay strewn over every stack in the storage area. The confusion of colors made his head hurt. *Heavenly Father, please tell me I'm dreaming.*

The early hour shed no light on the situation. The office harbored as many shadows as the pair of windows on the opposite wall. He lifted his lantern higher, rubbed his eyes, and took a second look.

Nope. His luck still hadn't changed for the better.

Another task had been heaped on his already mountain-high workload—and Grumpy Gus had to be the culprit. Why had his grandfather removed Miss Bell's belongings from their transport sacks? The cantankerous side of the old man had been appearing more often than his cooperative counterpart.

"Hellfire!" A fist of panic punched his heart. Had Gus wandered off again? If he reached the snowpack beyond the tree line, he might trigger an avalanche and plummet to—

"Is cursing how you say hello?"

The question came from the other side of the hills of rainbow shrouded freight where he now glimpsed the faint glow of another lantern.

"I know yer mother—God rest her sweet-as-sarsaparilla soul—taught you better 'n that."

His worry turned to relief, then frustration and finally acceptance. "Good morning." He aimed for a cheerful tone but he doubted if he'd have fooled a stranger, let alone someone who knew him as well as Gus.

"That's better but not great. I'm adding brushing up on yer manners to my list."

That Gus had a task list was nothing new. Jack had one as well. Lately Gus might've slowed down, but the drive to work hard ran deep in the Peregrine family.

The smell of brewing coffee wafted from the other side of the stacks where Gus remained hidden from view. As long as the old man was somewhere in the building, it was a better day than most. And today was no different than any other. Put family and their shipping business first. Ignore his compulsion to barricade his life against heartache.

Instead, he must lay his soul bare and do whatever was necessary—including getting married again.

A vision rose in his mind. His tiny bride standing below him with her chin held high, questioning him with eyes that hid as much as they revealed.

Wary but curious. Watchful. Like a colly bird.

No, smaller than a blackbird and full of contrasts. Black hair. Pale skin.

A tiny chickadee perched on the tip of his open palm. One false move and she'd take flight and never be seen again. He'd be left with only memories. Her unwavering regard had entranced him, but her smile had rocked his dreams.

"Bet Madame Bonheur is chomping at the bit to get those brides out of her girls' rooms."

Jack nodded. Miss Bell would be much safer and extremely more appreciated in his bed upstairs. He couldn't shake that thought in particular from his mind. He needed a wife and now that he'd met his bride he desired her as well.

A future full of misery loomed large. Miss Bell had agreed to be his wife, but now that she'd seen the town and him, could he convince her to actually marry him?

"First thing you gotta do," Gus said as if sensing his worry, or maybe sharing it, "is impress her with yer manners 'n sugar talk. Women like that stuff."

"*First*, I need to make my deliveries." And before he could, he had to clear the main row that divided their usually meticulously organized office. Then he could reach the shipment that arrived yesterday with the brides. Incoming freight was always deposited directly behind the postal counter for him to record and distribute—which he always did the day it arrived.

Yesterday, he'd been distracted. Today, his customers would be wondering why their orders were delayed. Now they'd have to wait even longer. The disruption of his routine ruffled his own cantankerous side. He had only himself to blame.

He'd been hooked by a woman as foreign as she was familiar. She could easily leave him and Gus in the lurch.

And the town too. He should've focused on his work. He hung his lantern on a hook and stomped toward the stacks. He bit back his growl of impatience and discomfort when his leg protested his vigor and reduced him to a hobble.

The cast-iron firebox door clanked shut, confirming Gus' position by the stove where he was most likely adding more kindling. "Gotta keep our home warm 'n inviting," Gus said. "Know we probably shouldn't be working on Christmas Day but—"

"We worked last Christmas."

"True," Gus replied, still remaining unseen on the other side of the room. "And the one before that, as well. So..."

The silence that filled the office made him more agitated than Gus' chatter. "So, what?" he prompted.

"So, fortune favors the early bird. You shoulda got up earlier."

"Agreed." He gathered the materials obstructing his path, taking care not to damage the mysteriously soft, delicate fabrics. Why did such things appeal to women? Surely a stronger, more resilient cloth was preferable?

If Miss Bell stayed, she could explain the desire for such finery to him and his customers. She'd be a valuable asset to the Peregrine business. His mother had passed when he was young, but he and his brother still had two parents. They'd been raised equally by their father and grandfather. Gus deserved a worry-free retirement—and a restful one, too.

"What time did you get up?" he asked.

"Never went to sleep." At the other end of the room, Gus' head finally rose above the freight. His red hair and beard puffed out around him like a windblown gnome. "What's taking you so long? Stop lollygagging 'n get yer backside over here."

"I'm trying." Since he'd recovered from his initial shock

of entering the office and his daydreams about Miss Bell, he hadn't stopped moving forward. Yes, his pace was slow but it was also practical. He fought the compulsion to tidy everything in his sight and only gathered the items in his path. "I'm being careful and—"

"Fussy 'n finicky. Today ain't a good day to be a stickler. Daylight's burning."

"It's December. The sun hasn't risen. I doubt anyone else has either."

"Don't matter. We gotta get you presentable 'n seal the deal with yer bride fast." He waved the coffee pot in the air.

Jack flinched as coffee sloshed over the spout. When it spattered on the floor instead of Gus, he heaved a sigh of relief but also increased his pace. He threw Miss Bell's belongings willy-nilly out of his way in order to reach Gus. His top priority had become getting the hot liquid out of Gus' hands before he burned himself.

When he reached the end of the now hastily cleared row, Gus set the pot down with a clunk on the stove's flat top, picked up two full cups, handed one to him and raised the other in a salute.

"We both need a cup of inspiration for what comes next. Come hell or high water, we're convincing Miss Bell yer a fine catch." He waggled his bushy brows. "We're gonna dazzle her. We're gonna sweep her off her feet. We're—"

"Slow down. We don't want to—" What? Smother her with their rustic attention and limitations? Save that for the marriage bed when she saw, and felt, the stump of his missing leg. He stared at the floorboards and tried not to grimace. "We don't want to spook her."

Gus cleared his throat gruffly. "Yer worrying me. You ain't cracked a smile since spring."

That was before he'd been told the truth about Lorena.

This was his fault. His constant brooding was weighing on Gus. The old man had launched a mission to see him happy as if he thought time was running out.

Jack couldn't envision a future without his grandfather. He forced a smile and grasped Gus' much-too-thin shoulder. "We got plenty of time."

"No, we don't." Gus seized his shoulder as well and their eyes locked. "And you know it as well as me, Sunny Boy."

The childhood name stole the air from his lungs. When had he last heard it? Before his father died and he'd lost his leg fighting to save him? Before Lorena disappeared? Growing up together, she'd called him Sunny Boy along with everyone else. He should've realized they had major problems when she began referring to him simply as *husband*.

Neither name fit him anymore. Maybe they never had.

Life had crushed the cheerful boy who'd once smiled as brightly as his sun-burnished hair.

Gus' gaze went eastward, toward the other end of town where Jack's new bride slept oblivious to the turmoil that awaited her—if she still agreed to his proposal. "Miss Bell is the answer to my prayers. Give her a chance 'n you'll see she's perfect for you."

In his dreams she was perfect, but not in his reality. His life was too battered and broken, too hard for a woman of her petite stature. "In my letters, I repeatedly warned of hard work and the need for a strong wife. Why did she agree to come here?"

"Don't look a gift horse in the mouth. We'll keep her safe. She won't go missing like Lorena."

Jack's hands clenched into fists. For years, he'd held onto the belief that Lorena was alive and would find her way back to him. Now both he and Gus knew the truth concerning his wife's disappearance. But Gus' mind refused to remember what the Braverys—a husband and wife team who specialized in hunting for lost loved ones—had discovered.

"Surely Miss Bell received dozens of better proposals in Denver."

"Their loss is our gain." Gus gave him a disgruntled look. "Young men don't know how to hold onto an opportunity."

"I'm not that young."

"From where I'm standing, yer a spring chicken. So is Miss Bell. Yer an excellent match."

When she'd written that she was thirty—the same age as him, he'd deemed it as a good omen. They'd both had time to mature and outgrow any flighty behavior. If Miss Bell had any wild days, hopefully they were long behind her.

"A tenacious man wins the day," Gus said.

"It's not entirely up to the man. The woman has a say." Why had Miss Bell said yes to marrying him, a man she knew only from a few letters? She knew next to nothing about him.

"Miss Bell saw something in yer words. Now she's gonna see a helluva lot more in yer actions. Cause yer gonna pull out all the stops when courting her."

Jack leaned against the counter and rubbed his thigh. The newest wooden leg he'd carved fit better than the last one, but the stump of his lost limb still ached, especially before and after a storm—both ones created by the weather and his grandfather. From the corner of his eye, he watched Gus staring intently into his *cup of inspiration*. Once the old man latched onto a subject, he was as hard to shake free as a dog from your trouser leg.

He needed time to think before he faced Miss Bell and

Gus' advice on courting her. He knew he was avoiding the hardest part of his day, but he didn't care. He cast about for a way to distract Gus and himself.

His gaze skittered across their messy office and halted on Gus' leather stamping tools hanging neatly on the rack Jack had built as a Christmas gift their first year in Noelle.

"Why haven't you begun a new project?" He gestured with his chin toward Gus' tools. "Mayor Hardt and Hugh thanked you profusely for the briefcases you made for them. Woody loves the saddlebags. Culver's always using your tool roll. Kyi-yee's the same with the sheath for his hunting knife. And Draven's revolvers look extra deadly in your gun belt."

Gus shrugged one shoulder. "Making things ain't as easy as it used to be. So, I'm waiting."

"For?"

"Inspiration," Gus declared as if it should be obvious. "I want every item I create to be both unique 'n useful to its recipient."

"Why did you remove Miss Bell's *items*?"

"So they wouldn't get creased or stained inside those frost-bitten transport sacks. We had a devil of a storm yesterday, remember? Life is as unpredictable as the weather. You need to go visit Miss Bell *now*."

Jack pulled his watch from his pocket and considered the time. "Miss Bell will be tired from her travels and yesterday's excitement. She'll probably sleep till noon. I'll sort and deliver the town shipment, organize the office"—before she could see the chaos—"*then* I'll go see her."

"Don't forget to comb yer hair 'n shave before you do. You look like a wild man or a lion or the two rolled into one."

Jack raked his fingers through his tangled hair. It'd

always been too thick to be easily tamed. He had a lot to do before he was ready to face Miss Bell again.

A knock rattled the door. A foreign sound. If anyone in town saw a light in their window, they knew to open the door and let themselves in—even this early in the morning.

The knock came again. Louder. More determined, like bad news that couldn't wait.

With his nerves jangling, he crossed to the door and yanked it open.

Miss Bell stood outside with her tiny fist raised to knock again. Her lips parted on a silent gasp and her eyes widened as her gaze traveled over him.

Behind him, Gus said the words racing through his mind, words that held him frozen with dread at his bride's unexpected and much too early visit. "Have you come to tell my grandson that the wedding is off?"

CHAPTER 5

*B*irdie blinked in shock. The sight of Jack towering over her with a halo of lantern light behind him left her breathless. So did his grandfather's words.

Did they *want* her to call the wedding off? Why didn't the possibility please her? Getting tied down in marriage had been the cost of escaping Denver with her treasure trove of fabrics and partially made dresses. If she could find another way to solve her current predicament, she would've taken it. Wouldn't she?

Jack Peregrine remained stock-still, staring at her like he wanted to carry her upstairs and consummate their marriage immediately. Her eyes had to be deceiving her. Jack had yet to comment on his grandfather's question. She needed to discover the truth of the situation without revealing too much about her present or her past—which still held the power to destroy any hope of a normal future.

She dredged up a reply that answered but still avoided his grandfather's query. "I'm here because I saw a light in your window." In the unusually *high* windows that she hadn't been able to peek through and see what might await her inside.

She'd had to go forward blindly. Something she disliked doing. She lowered her hand and pressed her palm to her chest in an effort to calm her pounding heart.

A frown creased Jack's brow. "You saw our lantern all the way from *La Maison?*"

"No, of course not. I took a chance you'd be up and saw your light as I crossed the bridge." It had taken all of her willpower to walk serenely past the sheriff's jail on the main street. Her wish to never meet the man had influenced her early start. Hopefully Draven wasn't a morning person.

Jack's frown deepened. "You ventured out alone?"

"She shouldn't have done that." Gus' gruff words came closer but she still couldn't see him with Jack filling the doorway. "It's not safe."

"Safe or not, I did it," she replied, trying to soften the resentment edging her voice. It wasn't her fault she had to do everything on her own. "I've been alone since I was sixteen. That should prove I can take care of myself."

It was Jack's turn to blink in surprise.

She'd shared too much information and not the right kind. She was supposed to be a bride eager to end her solitude and find shelter under the wing of a man—this very large and handsome man standing before her.

Why wasn't he married?

Mrs. Walters had told Birdie that twelve marriages were required to provide an appearance of stability. The town needed to convince everyone it was prospering, not declining.

Was Jack's commitment to saving the town—and his freighting business—his primary reason for seeking a bride? The bleak thought didn't bode well for a loving union. Neither did Jack's disconcerting silences.

Before she could soften her reply and fill the void, Gus' words flew out as if a door to a birdcage had been opened, "What if you got lost? Being so new to Noelle, you might not find yer way back to us. You might wander for days, for years. You might—"

Jack spun sideways and clasped the old man's shoulder. "Miss Bell is fine. She made it safely to our office and she'll let us know when she's ready to leave. That way I can walk her back to *La Maison* or wherever else she wishes to go." His gaze cut back to her. "Won't you, Miss Bell?"

Normally she'd find a way to sidestep such a commitment. She disliked breaking promises that might prove impossible to keep. But the worry on Gus' face as he contemplated her—and on Jack's face as his gaze darted between her and his grandfather—made her say, "I'll let you know."

Jack gave her a thankful look, then raked his fingers through his hair. The restless gesture didn't soothe his wild mane. He'd need help for that. A woman's help. A wife's.

But he'd only sought one when this town decided their bachelors must wed to entice a railroad line to join with them. A thoroughly unromantic notion. An unfamiliar one, too. She was used to looking after only herself.

She'd do well to guard both her heart and her prospects in Noelle.

She scanned her surroundings for a way to steer the conversation in a new direction. Since she still couldn't see beyond the Peregrine men she was left with a view of the outside of their establishment. "You have a lovely office. I couldn't miss the sign's precisely carved lettering. The walls appear snuggly framed and the awning pleasantly minimizes the snow on your porch."

But those darned high windows were still a mystery and a nuisance.

She craned her neck to see around Jack and his grandfather, curious to glimpse what lay inside and answer a question that pestered her since the wagon driver had parted her from her possessions—was her treasure trove of fabrics and partially made dresses safe in the Peregrines' care?

"I imagine it's quite cozy inside," she added.

Gus coughed gruffly while at the same time saying something that sounded like, "Manners."

"My apologies." Jack stepped aside and gestured for her to enter. "You must be cold. Please come in."

Her gaze clung to him as she crossed the threshold. Despite leaving the chill outside, she shivered as she leaned toward the heat radiating from him. "Winter is an old friend, so the cold doesn't bother me all that much especially since I made this coat." When she gestured to the garment, her fingers almost brushed Jack's chest. She tore her gaze and her hand away from him, and straightened her course. "I grew up in the snow, far to the east in—"

The sight of her fabrics and dresses covering a waist-high counter and everything on the other side halted her. It was a good thing. She'd been about to mention Quebec.

Her unusual giddiness at seeing Jack again had made her speak before weighing her words. Something she also disliked doing. It was never wise to give out too many details about a past one wished to keep secret. It was better for everyone to assume she'd been born in France.

The door closed behind her with a soft but resounding click.

Jack's breath brushed her ear as he walked by her and whispered, "I apologize for the mess as well, Miss Bell."

The mess was puzzling but she was thankful it had appeared and cut off her blathering. Then again having her inventory out of its bags meant she couldn't get everything in a wagon for a speedy departure. That was no longer an option.

The growing likelihood of losing her fabrics loomed like a black cloud with only one bright spot. It'd cover her debt.

Same as the other grooms, Jack had paid for the train ticket necessary for the first leg of his bride's journey to Noelle. But unlike the other men, he'd also invested his time and money to transport her inventory. When he found a buyer, her debt would be cleared. He'd temporarily be out of pocket.

Guilt shouldn't prick her conscience, but it did. Finding a replacement bride to meet Jack's needs, and the town's as well, wouldn't be so easy. She must harden her heart against dwelling on such concerns.

The Peregrine men had moved to a potbelly stove set against the wall. Gus poured a cup of coffee and held it out to her. Jack grabbed the back of a chair and turned the seat toward her.

"Come sit by the stove and warm yourself," he said.

Her fingers itched to hold a needle and resume work on one of her dresses, but her feet obeyed Jack's words and went straight to him. Luckily the cup Gus offered snagged her attention before she almost ran into his grandson again.

"Thank you," she said as she took the cup and sat down.

Jack guided Gus into the chair beside her with a well-practiced maneuver. The care he exhibited toward his grandfather warmed her more than the cup of coffee or the stove.

He leaned back against the counter and ran his hand down his left thigh. When he noticed her watching him, he hastily folded his arms across his chest but didn't look away. His gaze remained on her. So, did his grandfather's.

Both men ignored the elephant in the room. An awkward moment passed. A perplexing one too. She found her gaze flitting more to Jack than her fabrics and dresses behind him.

"Mr. Peregrine..." She drifted off, unsure what she wanted to say.

"Yes?" Both men said at once.

Jack laughed a deep alluring rumble. "It might be simpler if you use our given names."

Gus shook his head vigorously. "You can call him whatever you want, but I won't be happy unless you call me Grandpa. Yer part of the family now."

Family. She couldn't lie to herself anymore. That enticement—as much as the need to elude the Braverys—had brought her to Noelle and the Peregrines. But she was a long way from being part of this family. Vows had yet to be said or even mentioned.

Jack's frown returned when she remained silent.

"You are very kind. Jack. Grandpa." She nodded to each man in turn.

Gus' grin grew a mile wide as he winked at his grandson.

Seeing him so happy delighted her as well. "I hope you'll call me Birdie," she added.

"That's a pretty name." Jack said quickly as if trying to avoid another silence in their conversation. "Is it short for something?"

The familiar question shouldn't have made her heart race, but it did. She summoned an equally familiar reply along with the silent mantra: *answer, avoid, ask another ques-*

tion. "It is, but I've been called Birdie for so I long it's the only name I recognize. Did the canvas bags holding my belongings rupture?"

Jack stiffened. "No, but it's still my fault. I—"

"He slept in," Gus interrupted, "and I took action."

"How can you find anything with your office in this...condition?"

Jack released a weary sigh. "I can't."

"*Je suis désolée.*" The words slipped out before she could stop them.

"The matchmaker, Mrs. Walters, wrote that you were French." Jack cocked his head and studied her curiously. "But I only hear the hint of an accent. Are you—?"

"I'm apologizing," she said quickly. The last thing she wanted to do was talk about where she'd learned to speak her native language. "My arrival has caused you an inconvenience."

He shrugged. "Don't worry. It's only temporary."

His choice of words pricked her nerves. Was she also temporary? The Peregrines had been exceedingly courteous to her so far. Was Jack searching for a kind way to say he no longer wished to marry her? But the town still needed married men and the state of the Peregrines' office told her they needed her as well.

"When my grandson learned from yer letters that you were bringing the tools of yer trade, he built that for you." Gus gestured to a wooden shelf with many cubbyholes—all empty.

Her heart skipped a beat. "You built something for me?"

Jack frowned at his creation. "I should've known to make it bigger, and I haven't had time to add any drawers. It can be improved."

Eager to take a closer look, she left her chair and strode

to the gap in the counter. And abruptly halted. They'd progressed to first names and less stilted conversations, but she was still a stranger here.

She turned to Jack who now stood gazing down at her with both a hungry and mystified look.

"May I enter your office?" she inquired.

His eyebrows shot up in surprise. "You may go wherever you please. This is your home now."

Home. Could it really be within her grasp after all this time?

Her mouth went dry, so she murmured a quick thank you, set her cup on the counter and went to the shelf. Beneath her palms the wood had been sanded to an exquisite smoothness by Jack's strong but careful touch. "It's magnificent." She slid her arms into the cubbyholes, measuring. "My fabric bolts will fit perfectly. This is tailor-made. How did you know the dimensions?"

"I wrote to Mrs. Walters for advice."

Gus puffed out his chest. "Jack's creations are always useful 'n unique. He gets that from me."

"You've both been blessed with a great talent. Is this"— she swallowed hard—"a wedding gift?"

"It's a Christmas present." Gus pointed to the wall opposite her shelf. "Jack made this tool rack for me 'n keeps adding to it every year. He got tired of my tools being scattered everywhere 'n now I can do my leather tooling while I watch the postal counter."

The talk of gift making and giving had her scanning her inventory strewn about the office. Somewhere in the chaos were the scarves she'd made for Jack and one other. When he'd written that he had a family business, she'd decided to plan ahead and create a second matching gift for a potential relative. Since she hadn't known anyone's measurements, she'd chosen to make scarves. But she'd also chosen her softest, warmest, and most treasured red flannel.

When she glanced at Jack, she found him frowning at his office again.

"Where are your carpentry tools?" she asked, wishing to distract him.

"I have a separate room in the back."

She glanced in the direction he'd indicated. "Do you work there every day?"

"I try to, but lately my time has been needed elsewhere."

"A lot of folks left Noelle," Gus said. "They needed our help transporting their belongings. My younger grandson, Max, saw a business opportunity 'n opened a Peregrines' Post and Freight in Denver."

"We have plenty of work here." Jack pressed his lips tight and stared at the ceiling.

"We're still a family business," Gus said firmly. "A little distance won't change that. Max needed to spread his wings. He hasn't left us."

Jack's gaze went everywhere but toward his grandfather and her.

The thought of leaving these two men suddenly made her heart hurt. Whatever happened tomorrow, she would embrace today. "What is a freight office's usual routine?"

"People give us their orders and I compile a list for Woody Burnside to take to Denver. He uses my mules to bring back the goods."

"How often do you make the supply run?"

"Me? Never."

Jack's vehement tone made her eyes widen.

"I pay Woody to do all the work associated with the mules. He's the best man for the job."

"You oughta forgive them beasts," Gus muttered.

"I don't understand. Why do you say—?"

"Despite my profession, I'm not fond of mules. Haven't been since the war. I do my part though by checking incoming items for inconsistencies or damages, reordering if necessary, and recording everything. Above all"—Jack's voice, which had grown lighter with recounting what he did do, suddenly turned strained again—"I strive to place every item in the hands of its owner as soon as possible."

Gus snorted. "He's a stickler for details 'n organization."

"Customers appreciate those qualities."

"You never stop working."

"It's how I keep our family together."

The Peregrines' rapid-fire exchange made her head spin and her stomach drop. "My arrival has interrupted your schedule and your lives."

Both men's gazes shot to her and their expressions turned guilty.

"Yer arrival takes precedence," Gus stated. "My grandson will escort you to Nacho's Diner for a meal while I handle the office."

"Nacho's isn't open this early, and you've been up all night *handling* things," Jack muttered and then said just as firmly as his grandfather, "Now it's my turn. Miss Bell, will you—"

"We agreed to call each other by first names." Her words came out before she had time to consider them. Suddenly she didn't care. She may be an interruption but she refused to be *handled*. She crossed her arms and braced for a fight.

Jack's expression remained stubborn. "Yes, we did. You also agreed to something else. Birdie, may I walk you to your accommodations and call on you when we've all had a chance to get settled and"—he waved his hand in the air as if searching for the right word to persuade her—"rested?"

She planted her hands on her hips. "Do I look tired?"

He scrubbed his fingers across his brow. "I just thought that with the early hour and—"

"Perhaps you should take a closer *look*."

Finally, he did. She expected him to scan her entire frame but his gaze stayed on her face.

"You look hale and hearty." His shoulders relaxed as if relieved by his discovery. He nodded and added. "And determined."

She cleared her throat uneasily. "And how do you feel about that trait?"

"I admire it greatly."

His compliment made her cheeks burn. "So why don't I stay and help get your routine and your office back to normal?" She leaned closer to him and whispered, "While your grandfather rests."

A breathtaking smile curled his lips. Even better, he reached out his hand. "Shall I hang up your coat so we can get to work?"

She held her breath, hoping for another compliment as she removed her coat and gave it to him. He took it without a word and placed it on a peg by the door.

She smoothed her palms down the dress she'd specially made for this moment, for impressing her groom with her handiwork. Her sapphire silk dress was covered in tiny silver birds. The closest thing she could find to a peregrine.

She waited for him to notice.

"That's an interesting contraption 'round yer waist," Gus said. "What is it?"

"My sewing chatelaine." Her hand went to her mother's scissors first, then the sketchpad and pencil—each secured by a woven ribbon triple-stitched to a brocade sash. When she reached her sewing case, she unrolled the foot-long band of velvet and showed him the contents. "Pins, needles, thread, a thimble. I carry the essentials for a quick mend."

"Yer a gem," Gus proclaimed as he slapped his knee. "You've made yer own tool belt."

She couldn't help but smile. In the absence of Jack's praise, his grandfather's was most welcome. "I never wish to meet the world unprepared."

"We should all be so wise." Gus left his seat by the stove and went to his own tools hanging on the wall opposite her shelf.

Jack followed and maneuvered Gus onto the stool behind the post office end of the counter. When he observed her watching him, he crossed to her side and once again bent to whisper close to her ear. "Don't worry about making noise. Once he drifts off he's hard to wake. Shall we make the most of our time together?"

CHAPTER 6

*M*any hours later, around midday, Gus was sleeping with his head and arms on the postal counter, and she and Jack had filled every inch of the shelves he'd made for her. The fabric that hadn't fit had been arranged atop the nearest stacks of freight, neatly and by color. She'd found the Christmas gifts she'd made for Jack and now Gus, but a sudden surge of anxiety made her hide them in a corner of the bottom shelf.

Jack hadn't mentioned the dress she wore. What if he didn't like it? What if he didn't like the gift she'd made for him as well? The joy of giving shouldn't be this nerve-wracking. She'd do well to wait a while and see what came next before offering her gifts.

Jack's silence concerned her, but luckily not as much as it first had.

She'd enjoyed her time working beside him and the fact that whenever she glanced at him, she found his gaze on her more often than not. Suddenly that felt better than words.

She watched him string a line of cord from the ceiling

and hang her partially made dresses on it. They formed a colorful but orderly backdrop. When he adjusted the line, so she could reach it, her heart melted and then she laughed.

"Oh, Jack. What's happened to your hair?"

He frowned and glanced up. "How bad is it?"

"It's gotten even wilder since I arrived." She reached up but stopped short of touching him. "I could help here as well."

He leaned down until her fingertips brushed his hair.

Her fingers eagerly slid into his hair and didn't stop their combing. "You've been very neglectful in keeping this lovely mane in order."

He cocked one brow and a faint smile tugged the corner of his mouth. "Lovely?"

"That's what I said."

When he leaned even closer, his breath heated her cheek. "Shall I tell you what I think is lovely?"

"A tidy office," she teased. Her voice sounded breathless to her ears.

"You—standing so close to me."

The screech of the front door opening jolted them apart. A gust of frigid air rolled in along with a peacock of a man dressed in a striped suit. Maybelle Anderson, the bride who'd tried to make herself the center of attention yesterday during the women's arrival, strutted by his side. On the journey up the mountain and last night in *La Maison*, she'd bragged about everything in her life, including the fact that she was marrying the best man in town—a forward-thinking scholar, a king of words, a newspaperman named Horatio P. Smythe.

"I knew this day would come." The man pressed his palm to his chest just below his silk cravat and struck a pose like a dime novel hero braced to fight a great calamity.

The certainty that Birdie now faced the newspaperman raised her hackles. Men like him had helped lure her brothers to their doom. A reporter looking for a story had promised fame if they captured and detained the legendary fugitive tracker, Jellon Jerome. The deed had only led to her brothers' surefire arrest by the man's up-and-coming protégé, Lachlan Bravery.

"You have finally been derelict in your duties," Mr. Smythe proclaimed.

"We're no longer in the army." Gus sat upright behind the counter. He arched one brow mockingly. "Oh, wait, you never were, Horatio. Now there's a dereliction of duty."

"Why don't you sit by the stove, Mr. Smythe," Jack said in a stilted but still civil tone, "while I find—"

"My *duty* has always been to stand above the masses as a shining star of virtue." Horatio thrust out his chest. "That, of course, is something that a senile old coot and a less than whole man shall never understand."

Jack surged toward Horatio with a growl that mirrored her outrage.

She caught his arm. "I'm certain," she said in a soothing tone, "that the most honorable men in the room are the owners of the establishment."

Everyone gaped at her, including Jack. She followed his gaze straight to her hand on his arm. Beneath her palm and a layer of warm flannel, his muscles bunched and grew even harder. When she released him, he flinched.

Horatio's waxed mustache did little to conceal his condescending smile. "The top men know how to take charge. Give orders and such to their underlings."

"This is a family business," Jack replied as he rummaged

around the stacks nearest the postal counter. "I remind you of that every time you visit. We're all equals here."

"Hardly. Your brother always deferred to you." Horatio gestured to her shelf. "And now I see you've installed a woman in his place."

Birdie sealed her lips against inquiring what he meant. It would only give the windbag more fuel for criticism.

Maybelle's strutting steps approached her side of the office. When the woman leaned over the counter separating them, her strong perfume made Birdie sway in the opposite direction—as far from the woman as she possibly could without appearing rude.

"How can you stand it?" Maybelle asked in a voice dripping with pity. "This room is so austere but also crammed full. Like being smothered in a prison."

"You couldn't be more wrong." The chief cause of her suffocation was Maybelle's heavy-handed application of fragrance. She kept her gaze fixed on Jack. "If you looked closely, you'd see—"

Jack muttered a curse and swung to face Gus. "Have you seen yesterday's shipment?"

"What odd windows." Maybelle's unwelcome words came closer to her ear. "Their height restricts the view."

Birdie couldn't argue that point but she could ignore Maybelle in favor of focusing on the events unfolding across the room.

"I thought the wagon driver brought it in yesterday with..." A puzzled frown furrowed Gus' brow. "With Miss Bell's items."

"He did." Jack turned in a circle. "Any ideas about where the shipment could be *today*?"

"This situation is unbearable," Horatio proclaimed.

Maybelle seized Birdie's wrist and released a dramatic

shudder. "These windows must be *unbearable* for someone of your reduced stature."

"You're wrong again, Maybelle. It didn't take me long to feel comfortable here. Then your groom arrived and—"

"This is a travesty," Horatio's booming declaration cut her off.

"It's a delay," Jack shot back. "They happen but not very often in Peregrines' Post."

"It should never happen to me. I am an important man. I need to pick up my last shipment before I can—" Horatio's words halted as abruptly as Maybelle's posturing. The pair stared at each other for an uncomfortably long moment.

"What's yer rush?" Gus demanded.

"Never mind," Horatio said. "Just find my box."

Gus folded his arms. "Not until you remember that you agreed, same as my grandson, to get hitched and be one of the twelve couples presented to the railroad inspector by January sixth. That's the deal."

Birdie barely suppressed her gasp. She hadn't been informed of a deadline. Did Mrs. Walters know?

Gus glared at Horatio. "You promised you'd save Noelle."

"I have *saved* this town a thousand times with my reporting. Tomorrow's paper should recommend that you be court-martialed for this blunder. If my box is lost—"

"It's inside this room." Jack's rigid tone matched his stance. "I'll find it."

Birdie yanked free of Maybelle's grasp and rushed to his side. "I'll help you. What kind of box are we looking for?"

The tension in Jack's shoulders eased. "A small blue one."

Horatio huffed in indignation. "A travel case's small size is part of its grandeur. This particular gentleman's grooming set is a work of art. Each piece is crafted from ornate French Guylock."

"*Guilloché*," Birdie corrected.

Horatio scowled at her. "What?"

"The pronunciation is *Guilloché*."

"Whatever. The box is priceless. The hand mirror itself is worth hundreds."

Priceless but he could still assign a dollar value. Birdie strove to keep her expression neutral.

"What if someone stole it?" Horatio demanded.

Birdie fought another battle not to fidget when his stare stayed on her. Was he insinuating that she'd done the deed?

Horatio's gaze went to the empty spot beside him. He blinked as if startled until his skittering gaze found Maybelle. "What are you doing so far away from me?"

She made a grand show of sashaying back to his side and linking her arm with his.

"Much better." He gave her hand a primly awkward pat. "Now, tell me, did you see a bride behaving suspiciously on yesterday's journey?"

Maybelle's chin rose to a haughty angle. "Most definitely."

"Which ones?"

"All of them."

"Oh, the travesties abound!" Horatio clutched his chest in horror, but his eyes shone with glee. "If I were not so busy a man, I would report their deplorable behavior in my paper as well."

"You are too good for this town, Horatio."

"I tell myself that at least a dozen times a day."

Horatio and Maybelle maintained a constant stream of conversation while she and Jack searched.

Jack handed her a small bag of letters. "Can you put

these in the top drawer directly behind you? We'll sort them later."

When she opened the drawer, a shiny enamel box—the color of a robin's egg—lay there.

"Jack," she said in a hushed voice, not wanting to alert Horatio to her find. "Is this—?"

"Has it been there the entire time?" Horatio boomed like a cannon as he reached across the counter for the box.

Jack shoved a leather-bound journal between the man and his target. He flipped it open and jabbed the page with his index finger. "You know the rules. Sign the ledger first."

Gus snorted a laugh. "My grandson's a stickler for details. You should appreciate that, Horatio."

With a flamboyant flourish, the newspaperman wrote his name.

"It is a beautiful box," Birdie remarked, wishing to fill the stilted silence. "A calming blue."

"A royal blue fit for a king."

Birdie bit her lip against correcting him again.

"Isn't that a darker, more vibrant shade?" Maybelle surveyed her with sudden envy. "Like the color of her dress."

Horatio's Adam's apple bobbed as if he realized his mistake. "My box," he stated loudly, "is a hundred times more regal than the vulgar pattern on her dress."

Birdie flinched liked she'd been cut. It'd been a long time since anyone criticized one of her creations, especially one she wanted so desperately to find favor.

"You're right, of course," Maybelle rushed to say. "My vision was overpowered by the dreary clutter of my surroundings."

"One too drab. The other too showy." Horatio stared down his nose at her as he stroked his mustache.

It wouldn't take much to clip his arrogance. Seamstresses often made good barbers. Her hand went to the scissors waiting in her sewing chatelaine.

"The only thing more beautiful than Miss Bell's dress," Jack replied in the firm tone he'd eventually come to use with his grandfather, "is Miss Bell."

Birdie felt her jaw drop along with Horatio and Maybelle's.

"You are lucky you found my box." Horatio steered Maybelle toward the door. "I was a heartbeat away from reporting you to Sheriff Draven."

The air in Birdie's lungs vanished.

Jack slammed the door closed behind the departing pair. She clutched the counter to stop herself from leaving as well. If she ran out, she'd definitely get the attention she craved from Jack—but for the wrong reason.

Gus patted her shoulder. "Ignore Horatio. He's all bluster 'n no substance."

Jack moved to the window. He was the perfect height to see what she could not. "I need to talk to Draven before our newspaperman, or someone else, does."

Birdie gasped in disbelief. "But your grandfather said—"

"I keep forgetting things," Gus interrupted in a glum voice. "Like this family doesn't need another thief making a mess of things."

"Grandpa," Jack said with a sigh. "Nothing has been stolen, and messes can be cleaned up. Look at how Birdie helped tidy our office and find Horatio's box. The most important thing is that we work together."

How could he talk so calmly? Even an accusation of dishonest behavior could ruin a person's standing in a community. The Peregrines' fortunes could plummet as quickly as hers had.

Jack went back to searching the stacks of freight. "We'll find the rest of the Christmas Eve shipment."

The news that they hadn't found everything sent a chill up her spine. "How much more is missing?"

"Only a handful of small items. Their size is probably why we haven't located them. But they're in this office. Somewhere." His perplexed frown was at odds with his confident tone. When he glanced her way, and found her staring at him, he gave her a reassuring smile. "I'm not concerned and neither should you be."

The worry lines on his face told her differently.

She pulled a random dress from the line, claimed a seat by the stove, threaded a needle, and sought her own serenity. Making a dress usually settled her nerves and allowed her to see a way forward. If she could concentrate on her work, her path might become clear again.

Jack's footsteps came toward her and stopped by her side.

She didn't look up. She kept sewing and struggling to breathe normally.

"I couldn't have tackled today without you, Birdie. Thank you."

His kind words made her throat tighten. She had to swallow several times before she could speak. "I'm always glad when I can help."

"Would you like to..." his voice lowered to a husky murmur, "...join me for a meal at Nacho's Diner now?"

She shook her head. "I need to finish this dress."

"You need to eat eventually as well."

"Maybe later."

"You found a buyer for the garment? That was quick." He edged a step closer to her.

Probably to get a better look at her handiwork. It'd be foolish to crave something else.

"Is that why you need to complete it now?" he asked.

Why was he suddenly so interested in a dress? And why had he only commented on the one she wore after Horatio had insulted it? He'd called her beautiful. Was she merely a possession that a man needed to defend and parade on his arm like doll? She'd seen too many of those women pass through her dress shop in Denver.

Not for the first time, she wished she had a friend she could talk with freely. Other than Jack and Gus, the only people in Noelle whom she'd had a genuine conversation with were Mrs. Walters and Pearl. Maybe Pearl being a resident of Noelle could explain Jack's behavior. Even if Pearl couldn't, it'd be a relief to share her worries. Not all of them of course, but a few.

"I'm not selling this dress. I'm giving it away."

"That's very kind of you. Who's the lucky lady?"

"Hopefully a new friend." If she told him she wished to win Pearl's friendship, would he forbid her from attempting to befriend a fallen woman? Many people considered them no better than thieves and their abettors. Unredeemable souls. Like the Bellamy family.

"What do you mean by hopefully?"

"Why are you badgering me with so many questions?" She tried to sew faster. She needed to finish this dress and get back to *La Maison*. She pricked her finger on her needle and winced.

Jack captured her hands and held her still. "Birdie, please slow down. I know Gus and I aren't a perfect family but if you give us a chance, I promise I'll look after you. I want you to eat and rest. I need you to stay strong."

She waited for him to mention vows and marriage.

When he didn't, she pulled her hands from his. "What did Horatio mean when he said you'd installed me in your brother's place?"

"Max makes his own creations. He worked on them beside Grandpa Gus while I labored in my carpentry shop. Your shelf replaced the one I built for Max. That's all."

Of course! This was why he hadn't spoken of their marriage since her arrival. She'd misread the way he'd studied her. Jack only wanted her as a helpmate for his business and his grandfather. He didn't really want to marry her. But he'd have to save the town and his livelihood.

She bowed her head to hide the tears stinging her eyes, and hugged the dress tight. All she had was her work. She rose to her feet. "It's time I returned to *La Maison*."

The dress could be completed there just as easily as here. Then what? She didn't want to run out of work distractions, so she gathered a selection of fabrics and notions that might form a dress for Kezia's sweet baby Jem.

Jack frowned at the load in her arms. "Let me carry that for you. We're walking together, remember?"

She'd promised she'd do that. She donned her coat quickly. Jack pulled his on much more slowly. As soon as he got the door opened, he reached to take the items from her arms.

He also cast a worried look at Gus.

Outside on the street, she glimpsed a pair of brides heading the way she needed to go. "I'll walk with them. That way I won't be alone and neither will your grandfather."

His arm shot out to block the doorway and her escape. "Are you running away from me, Birdie?"

She wished he'd wrap his arms around her and never let go. She shook her head, rejecting her foolish longings.

His voice lowered to a husky whisper as he leaned closer

to her. "Tell me that you want me to come and visit you tomorrow at *La Maison*."

"You ask for too much." She ducked under his arm and raced away before he could stop her from joining the brides who, unlike her, still had the hope of adding love to their lives.

CHAPTER 7

The 2nd day of Christmas
December 26, 1876

*B*irdie raised the hood of her coat, bowed her head and plowed into a chill headwind as she left *La Maison* and slogged through the snow toward Peregrines' Post. She clutched her newest creation against her chest when another stab of unease pricked her conscience.

Her mother's words rose from her memories along with a dusting of snow disturbed by her strides. *Sewing while upset often results in unwelcome creations.*

No turning back now.

At least her sewing had calmed her enough to face another day in Noelle. Or maybe it had been Jack's question about running away from him. Her feet may have scurried to *La Maison* but her entire body balked at going any farther.

In the early morning, the street was shrouded by slowly brightening skies over a blanket of white. A peaceful vista but not hushed like yesterday. A deep rhythmic pounding beat like a drum, echoing down the street from the higher ground at the mine.

She breathed easier when she once again passed the jail without incident. By Cobb's Penn, the dry goods store, she glimpsed a thin figure peering in the window. A puff of red hair tipped in white frost shone like a beacon below the man's flat cap and above his raised collar.

She angled her course to join Gus. She was glad to see him and have an excuse to stop and catch her breath. "Good morning, Gus—I mean, Grandpa. You're out early today. What are you shopping for?"

He shot her a glance then turned back to the window. His usual grin from yesterday was absent. "I'm late, aren't I?"

"For what?"

"Escorting you to our office. I somehow ended up talking to Doc Deane." He gestured over his shoulder. "His clinic is across the street."

A worried frown pinched her brow. "Is everything all right with—" She'd been about to say "your health," but stopped herself in time. Gus probably got pestered about his well-being more than he liked. "The doctor appeared flustered the day we came to town. How is he today?"

When they'd arrived at the saloon on Christmas Eve, she hadn't known that Noelle had a doctor. She'd learned about Doctor Deane after she'd watched him greet his bride, the flame-haired Cara Donnelly, by kissing her twice and calling her darling. He'd also called her by a different last name.

"Doc must have woman challenges," Gus replied. "That explains our peculiar conversation a moment ago. He shoulda asked for my advice or spoke to my grandson. Jack has everything firmly in hand."

Surprise held her momentarily speechless. "Jack said that?"

"He agreed that he needed to brush up on his manners, 'n that it ain't a good time for anyone to be out alone."

And yet Gus had stood alone on the street gazing in the shop window.

"Did Jack say anything else *this morning*?" Or had Gus wandered out without a word again?

When Gus didn't answer her question, she stomped her feet to shake off the snow and warm her toes. "I haven't seen a winter like this in a long time." A pair of snowshoes inside the store had her pressing her nose eagerly against the glass. She hadn't worn them since her youth. They would make walking in the snow much easier.

"The drifts get deepest beyond the trees. You shouldn't go there. Or so Jack is always telling me. We'd best get back to him." Gus offered his arm gallantly, but his expression remained subdued.

With their arms linked, she slowed her pace to match Gus' as they trudged together through the snow toward Peregrines' Post. What had he been thinking about to make him stare so intently in the store window? And how firm were Jack's hands for handling *women challenges*?

The last question made her jittery with anticipation and anxiety. She summoned a smile and said, "It must be disconcerting having this many women descend upon a town."

"The more women the better."

"Even women like Maybelle?" she queried, hoping to coax a smile from him.

She was rewarded with a belly laugh.

Gus' delight continued as he winked at her and patted her hand. "Yer sweet but you also got sass. I like that. But everyone's different. I appreciate that as well. Even if I don't always say so. Standing outside the store, I was recalling how my Willa loved peppermint but our daughter, Ginny, hated it. I once had as many women around me as men."

Her heart ached for his loss. She wasn't the only one missing family. "Oh Grandpa, I wish— I wish life were kinder."

"Me too. But that starts with people. Unfortunately, too many are like Maybelle 'n Horatio."

She strove for a lighter topic. "What's your advice for a happy marriage?"

His back straightened like a well-trained soldier as he said, "Listen to yer wife. Do as she says. She's always right." His posture relaxed as he paused. "Or at least my Willa was. As were Ginny and her friend, Esther, who married our son, George, and gave us Jack and Max. I was never sure about Lorena though."

"Who is Lorena?"

"She was...different as well."

His vague answer made her study him closely as she waited for him to say more. When his whole body sagged, she clutched his arm tighter.

"The good Lord took them from us much too early," he whispered.

She'd experienced no victories for keeping loved ones safe. All she knew how to do was take care of herself. She opened her mouth, wanting to say something to ease Gus' worries, but he spoke before she could.

"I won't let anything bad happen to you." Gus tightened his hold on her as well. "Now, watch yer step. It's slippery here sometimes."

Here being the porch of Peregrines' Post and Freight. The walk had gone quickly with Gus by her side.

The door flew open and Jack filled the doorway, once again looking wild-haired but better than any man had a right to—especially at this early hour. His frown turned to wide-eyed astonishment when he saw her. "You came back." He glanced at Gus and heaved a sigh. "And you found him."

Gus snorted. "*I found her* because I went looking for her."

"I asked you to wait here until I—"

"You were moving too slow."

"I was preparing breakfast. A task you insisted upon in case anyone"—his gaze cut briefly to her—"showed up unexpectedly. Then you slipped out *unexpectedly* and *alone* and—"

"Time alone can help with perspective," Birdie said, recalling her night at *La Maison* away from Jack, and other memories as well. "During the winter of my eleventh year, I walked two miles to school every day with only a pair of snowshoes for company."

Jack's lips parted in surprise as he stared at her.

She bit the inside of her mouth to keep from sighing or grimacing. It was a challenge not to do both. Speaking without thinking came from pondering the past too much while loitering outside shop windows.

A slow smile curved Jack's mouth as he propped his arm on the doorjamb and studied her. "Did you walk uphill both ways as well?"

Was he teasing her? "That doesn't seem likely."

"What if your home and your school were on hills with a valley separating them?"

She narrowed her gaze on him. "How often does that happen?"

He leaned even closer to her. "For other people, probably not often. But it was *my walk to school* when I was a boy in Kentucky."

She blinked in surprise. He'd shared a snippet of his past with her and his tone still sounded teasing and lighthearted and— Could he be flirting with her? She held her breath, waiting for him to say more.

"Can we continue this inside?" Gus grumbled. "It's cold out here. Not to mention Birdie would like her breakfast 'n I need my coffee."

She was only hungry for what Jack might say next.

He straightened to his full height and stepped aside so they could enter. The increase in the distance between them had her battling another sigh—this one of disappointment.

"The stove's nice and hot," Jack said. "Have a seat there and I'll serve you breakfast."

Courteous but not overly romantic. Still, the day was young. They had hours to talk.

When they were all inside, Jack gestured to the corner where a long wooden stick covered in carvings rested. "If you had to go out, Grandpa, why didn't you at least take your walking stick?"

Gus rolled his eyes. "'Cause I forgot 'n you didn't remind me earlier."

"What an interesting creation," Birdie remarked, trying to derail another argument. "Who made it?"

Gus raised his chin proudly. "We both did. Jack found the perfect branch 'n I used it to practice the carving Kyi-yee taught me."

Before she could ask who owned such a unique name, Jack's gaze fixed on the parcel in her arms. "Did you finish making your friend's dress?"

His question veered her course from the stove to the gap in the counter and through to her work area. Her doubts about her newest creation grew. She fought the urge to hide the parcel and its contents. Too late.

Why had Jack commented on it within seconds of

noticing it? Why couldn't he have said something just as early yesterday about her bird-patterned dress?

She set the parcel on the counter and summoned her mantra: *answer, avoid, ask another question.* "I was distracted last night and sewed...something else. I'll work on her dress today." She'd taken Pearl's measurements last night and an excellent match from her partially made dresses hung on the line. At least her idea to start as many garments as she could, with the hopes of finding the perfect owner later, was working out. "Did you sleep well last night?"

"No, I was distracted as well."

"By?" She tried not to stare at him too eagerly.

"Dreams."

Gus coughed and at the same time muttered what she was now sure was "manners."

Jack crossed to stand with only the counter between them. "Can I take your coat and hang it up for you?"

Her face heated both from his request and from continuing to wear her coat in the warm room. Jack had really stoked the fires today. He'd made her breakfast. He'd shared a story from his youth. He'd mentioned dreams. Above all, he was being exceedingly kind.

She pushed the hood from her head, but stopped there. Maybe she could keep her coat on all day and hide what lay beneath it. Or maybe Jack wouldn't comment on anything she wore or didn't wear today. Would that be any better? She craved his attention, his compliments. Maybe—

Mon Dieu! When had she become such an indecisive little mouse?

She raised her chin, removed her coat, and handed the garment to Jack. She also said what she hoped was a composed sounding, "Thank you." Then she took hold of the parcel waiting on the counter and forced herself to continue speaking. "I made curtains last night. With your permission, I'd like to hang them in your office."

"You don't have to ask. You can do whatever you like. As I said yesterday, this is your home now."

And still he made no mention of exchanging marriage vows. Instead he retrieved a stepladder from between two stacks of freight.

Yesterday, Felicity had married Reverend Hammond in a ceremony as surprising as it was joyful. Not to mention timely. A traveling judge had been in Noelle at the perfect moment to marry the eager pair.

Ils ont de la chance! Maybe their luck and happiness would flow her way today.

Jack cleared his throat, knocking her out of her hopeful musings. "I'll help you hang your curtains, if you like."

"That would be lovely." She opened the wrapping, draped the pleated panels over her arm, and joined him by the windows. "But we won't need a ladder for this." She tapped the wall directly below the glass. "Please put the top of the fabric here."

A furrow creased Jack's brow. "Seems like an odd place to hang a curtain. Don't they usually go over windows instead of under them?"

She shrugged. "Perhaps curtain is the wrong word. If I can't see out a window, I'd at least like to look at something colorful below the glass."

"Hellfire, I never thought about—"

"Language," Gus muttered.

Jack scrubbed his hand over the back of his neck. "Sorry for my cussing and my lack of foresight. Thought I was a better carpenter than this." He hung her curtains swiftly and exactly in the place she'd requested. When he stepped back to check his work, he sucked in a startled breath. "This is—" He reached for the fabric again but stopped short as if afraid to touch it now. "This *was* the dress you wore yesterday."

She attempted to keep her voice nonchalant as she said, "Some creations don't work out."

"Just like some days." He let his hand fall to his side. "I need to visit Sheriff Draven today."

She couldn't stifle her gasp.

Worry furrowed his brow as he spun to face her. "As I said previously, it's nothing to be concerned about. I should've gone yesterday, but I didn't want to," he lowered his voice, "leave Gus alone." His voice rose to its usual volume but his expression remained uncertain when he asked, "Will you both stay here until I return?"

Her heartbeat had slowed to a bearable rate, but her chest ached with the growing probability that she was falling into the role of caretaker rather than a wife. It would be a pleasure to spend more time with Gus, but after meeting Jack she wanted more.

So much more. A more she feared she'd never have with him—even if her luck held for the next few minutes and he wasn't visiting Draven to discuss her.

"Of course, I'm staying here," Gus said. "Where else would I go?"

A long list of possibilities unrolled in Birdie's thoughts.

Jack released a long-suffering sigh. When she remained silent, he leaned toward her. "Birdie, I need your help. I can't do this without you."

"Then I guess I'll be staying as well, but only until you return." She'd also be keeping the ladder by the window so she could stand on it and see the street. And she'd be sprinting out the back door if she saw Jack returning with the sheriff by his side.

CHAPTER 8

*C*arrying two packages of food, Jack strode down the street, hardly limping. Not having to run or even rush had allowed him to gradually loosen up his body. Knowing that Birdie was watching his grandfather, and Gus was watching his bride, had allowed him to do what he should've done yesterday.

Maybe he could finally catch up and not be a step behind where he needed to be.

He'd reported the missing items to Draven along with his suspicion that Gus had done the misplacing. Then he'd gone to talk to Doc Deane about Gus. The doctor had reminded him of the importance of food and sleep. He couldn't control Gus' sleeping patterns but he could make sure both Gus and Birdie never went hungry.

So he'd crossed the street and entered Cobb's Penn. Liam Fulton had been absent but his dry goods store had been in good hands. A whirlwind named Avis Smith had sold him every item on his list in a manner so swift she'd made his head spin. Despite the young woman's brisk to the point of frosty manner, he'd thanked her and said Liam was lucky to have her in his life.

She'd given him a look he couldn't decipher and started rearranging a shelf of food tins. He'd meant what he'd said. He hadn't a clue how she'd managed to find anything in the cluttered store.

She must be one of the brides, but how had she ended up with Liam? When they'd drawn straws to determine who'd receive a bride, Liam hadn't been one of the lucky twelve.

Pondering the whims of changing fortunes, he'd headed to Nacho's Diner and picked up a hot meal. Gus should be happy with the treat and the romantic gesture for Birdie.

He hoped she'd be pleased as well. After this morning's setbacks of having a home with windows too high for her to see out of and the loss of her pretty dress, he wanted to give her a reason to smile.

His pace quickened. Usually he walked faster heading home, impatient to get back to work and more recently to ensure Gus was safe. Today, his pace was driven only by Birdie. He hoped she'd be as happy to see his return as he'd be to see her again.

Liam strode down the street fast carrying his own package. As they passed each other, they raised their hands in greeting but did not stop. Liam had a business to attend, same as him. And they both had a woman they should wed. If Avis Smith married Liam, she might rearrange his life so completely that Jack would never again get goosebumps from the store's disorganization.

Thank the Lord, he'd regained an orderly office, and Gus and Birdie were safely inside, and seemed to enjoy each other's company. Getting along with Gus might help convince Birdie to stay with them.

Things were looking up.

He opened Peregrines' front door and froze. Gus and Birdie stood behind the counter in identical poses—spines stiff, arms folded across their chests, eyes glaring at each other.

"What's wrong?"

Gus slapped the counter with his palm. "She shouldn't have done it."

Birdie shrugged and strolled back to her end of the counter. "It is what business people do."

The sharp edge to her usually sweet-tempered voice left him gaping at her. He averted his gaze as he set the food by the stove. "What's that?"

"We sell things" Birdie replied.

Gus struck the counter again. "But that fabric was important to you."

"I have lots of fabric."

"Not with birds."

Jack's stomach twisted into a knot. Maybe he could convince her to turn the curtains back into a dress and—

"That doesn't matter. Mr. Fulton fancied only the curtains and I, similar to you Peregrine men, like matching people with creations they want."

Jack spun to the windows. Below them the walls were bare and stark. "No..."

"You were gone a long time," she said in a brittle tone.

Gus jabbed his finger at Birdie. "And you spent half of my grandson's absence standing on the stepladder staring out the window after him."

Birdie huffed. "You exaggerate. It was only a few minutes. I was adjusting the curtains."

"And after Liam took them?" Gus asked. "Why did you

climb up on the counter 'n sit there? So you could peer out the window again in search of—"

"Hush, Grandpa." Birdie's cheeks glowed pink.

"I will not."

"My actions were driven by a desire to see Noelle's natural beauty." Birdie paced in a tight circle, waving her hands in the air as she talked. "The trees although dusted with snow provide a cozy home for even the smallest of birds. And while my curtains, I mean *wall panels*, added color here, they did not fit in, just like—" She gulped in a breath and went very still.

Jack rushed to her side. "I'll go to Liam and buy them back."

"You will not! I sold them for a reason."

He reached out his hand to comfort her and change her mind.

She jerked away from him. "Why did you say this was my home?"

Dread squeezed his heart. Birdie's rising agitation reminded him of yesterday when he'd tried to stop her from leaving. She'd ducked under his arm and bolted. He lowered his arm and struggled to speak above the worry tightening his throat. "Because I hoped you'd stay with us. I still do."

"Then why are we arguing about curtains?" Her gaze cut to Gus. "Or where I sat and stood, and why?" Her tiny body shook like a leaf in a windstorm. "Why aren't you telling me what the sheriff said?"

He retreated one step, and then another. He needed to give her space so she wouldn't run from him again. "Draven told me not to worry. I'm saying the same to you. You're safe with me. Don't worry."

Birdie's stiffness eased a fraction and so did his.

He pointed to the packages he'd deposited by the stove. "After I visited Doc Deane, I picked up food from Liam's and Nacho's."

"Bet none of them men," Gus muttered, "are having this many challenges with their brides."

"Grandpa! That's enough. Let's—" He cast about for a way to regain their earlier harmony. "Let's sit *together* and have something to eat."

Birdie snatched a heap of purple fabric from the counter. "I have sewing to finish. I want to complete my friend's dress today."

He yearned to touch her, to reassure her with a gentle caress instead of blundering about with words. He kept his hands to himself and hazarded one last question. "Will you—?"

"I'm not doing anything until this dress is done. Even if it takes me all afternoon, I'm not budging from behind this counter."

He'd wanted to ask if she'd stay at Peregrines' Post for the day. She'd given him that, so he sealed his lips against saying anything more. They both needed to work. He had more tasks he should be keen to complete. But he wanted only to stay close to Birdie.

He forced himself to walk away from her. "I'm going to my carpentry shop for a while."

"Fine." Gus stomped toward his leather tooling rack. "I've got a project that needs my attention too."

Jack held no concerns about cornering his grandfather, right up against his tool rack. "Grandpa—" he whispered.

"Go on," Gus muttered. "I ain't leaving that gal's side." His voice dropped to an almost indecipherable grumble. "I'm protecting her from everyone—including you, me 'n herself."

Jack's feet didn't pause as he limped down the row dividing the stacks of freight. He couldn't keep his gaze from darting back in search of Birdie though. He only faced completely forward when he shut the door behind him and crossed his carpentry shop. He kept going.

Up the stairs. To the bedrooms above.

When he'd shared his sorry tale with Draven, the sheriff being a savvy man had simply asked if he'd searched the entire building, including Gus' room.

He raked his fingers through his hair and wondered not for the first time if he was losing his mind as well. Why hadn't he thought to do this right away? One last search. If he came up emptied-handed, he'd slog the back way into town. He wasn't disturbing Birdie or Gus again.

He'd visit his customers, explain the delay, apologize, ensure them it'd never happen again, and organize to reorder their items or refund their money.

He wasn't a thief. Neither was Gus. Horatio Smythe, or any newspaperman like him, would never truthfully be able to print that he or his kin had been associated with anything deceitful.

The Peregrines were an honest family, and he meant to keep it that way.

CHAPTER 9

*B*irdie pinned her completed dress on the line and sighed with satisfaction. If she were still in Denver, she could've sold the garment to any number of ladies. But this dress was meant for Pearl, in more ways than one. The shimmering amethyst silk would go divinely with the woman's blue eyes and blonde hair.

If Pearl had a worthy admirer, he should be wasting no time. He should be calling on her more frequently. She shook her head. This time her sigh was resigned.

Today the value of waiting and watching for revelations —like whether or not a man's affections ran deep—had become glaringly apparent. She'd been in Jack's home all day, but he'd spent only a few minutes with her. His interest had waned now that he'd set her up as his grandfather's minder.

At least he hadn't returned with the sheriff.

She should be glad. It'd make it easier to leave if—or more accurately when—the time came. No attachments. No family bonds. No husband eager for her company.

Even Gus had stopped talking to her. He once again

slept with his head on the counter. No wonder he didn't sleep at night.

Another creaking floorboard at the rear of the office made her gaze dart that way in the hopes Jack would appear. She'd been doing this all day.

Quelle idiote! The sound was merely the fading day's temperature drop making the wood complain.

But then the door at the rear opened, Jack limped in, and her world became vibrant again.

Gus lurched upright from his nap. The same as he had when Horatio and Maybelle had arrived yesterday. It seemed the one sure thing that could wake him was a door opening.

He rubbed his eyes as he asked, "What time is it?"

Jack consulted his pocket watch. "Suppertime."

Gus yawned. "When you feast at Nacho's tonight, be sure to ask him for a mug of that new chocolate milk concoction he let me taste yesterday."

Jack gave her an apologetic look. "There's no such drink. He didn't visit Nacho's yesterday. He was here all day."

The corners of Gus' mouth twitched as if he were suppressing a grin. "If you say so."

Jack's gaze narrowed on his grandfather. "You left without telling me?"

"Had to make a delivery." Gus drew himself up ramrod straight. "I am the postmaster, after all."

"Grandpa—"

Birdie cut Jack off before another argument exploded. "You've mentioned dining at Nacho's before. It's an unusual name. What does it mean?"

"Nacho is short for Ignacio. Mr. Villanueva's given name," Gus explained. "He's got fancy plates and mugs called Talavera and sweet bread he's dubbed *pan dulce.*"

Her heart leapt in anticipation of her and Jack sitting together in a restaurant with different food and furnishings. A change of scenery might rekindle the teasing tone he'd used this morning. Without the distraction of work, it might finally lead to a discussion about their marriage.

"Nacho also has a new bride," Gus added. "If she's livened up his menu or his life, I want to hear about it tomorrow."

"We can discuss it tonight because we're *all* going to Nacho's."

Jack's reply struck a discordant twang through her body. He'd turned their romantic dinner into a family outing. Would they ever get a moment alone together? Did Jack even want that?

Hounded by such questions, their meal promised to be long and dismal.

"Let's go." Gus elbowed Jack in the side and angled his head toward her coat.

She reached the door before he could and donned the garment without his assistance. With no sustained interest on his part, she'd do well to maintain her distance. If she accidentally touched him and he pulled away, she'd burn red with embarrassment.

When both men had their coats on, Jack paused with his hand on the door handle and gave his grandfather a tired but also determined look. "Aren't you forgetting something?"

"If I am, I'm sure you'll tell me. Eventually."

"Your walking stick?"

"Don't reckon I need it tonight or any night." Despite his words, Gus grabbed the stick and waved it at Jack. "But it's easier to take it than to argue with you about not taking it."

After they trooped outside and locked the door behind

them, they trudged in a row with her in the middle. Nobody touching. Everyone silent. If one didn't count Gus muttering under his breath as he stabbed the snowy ground with his stick.

The resonant but muted pounding that'd come from the mine all day now seemed unduly loud in the hushed silence outdoors. What caused the noise? Some sort of mining device, no doubt. Normally she would've asked what kind, but her gloomy mood had stifled her curiosity.

When they drew even with the Golden Nugget Saloon, Gus halted. "Time for us to part ways."

"What happened to going to Nacho's?" Jack asked in a weary voice.

"Did I say I was going?"

"You said *let's go*."

"I only did what was needed to get you within spitting distance of yer destination. And now that I have, I'm rewarding myself with a visit to the Nugget." With his stick propped on his shoulder, Gus beelined for the saloon's doors and disappeared inside.

Worry knotted Birdie's stomach. "Will he be all right?"

"Once he's in the saloon he usually doesn't come out till I drag him out. I'll do that on my way home."

"*Bonté divine!* He likes to drink that much?"

"He likes to talk that much."

She burst into laughter. It doubled her over and brought tears to her eyes. She couldn't stop. She didn't want to when Jack's laughter joined hers.

"Oh, I haven't laughed that hard in years."

"Same here," Jack replied with a grin that dazzled her. "I should clarify, though. Gus does enjoy a glass of beer and if he's drinking with Ezra Thornton, Storm's grandfather, he'll easily enjoy more than one."

"Your *grand-père* is..." She paused in search of the right word.

"A pain the backside."

"*Au contraire*. He is a pain in the everywhere. *C'est tout un fauteur de troubles.* Still, I appreciate his consistency and adore his moments of spontaneity even more."

"I enjoy seeing you relax when you speak French."

She shook her head. "To speak that language is unwise."

"How so?"

"Madame Bonheur has a French accent."

"Not like yours. Yours is beautiful, honest, real."

"Reality is complicated. The madam's entire life is artifice and mimicry." *We all do what we need to survive.* "Even her name is tricky. *Bonheur* means happiness. Or even good luck or fortune. I've heard that several of her girls took French-inspired aliases as well. Boum Boum, Jolie, Angélique."

"I've wondered about your name. Birdie Bell doesn't sound French. Isn't Bell an English or Irish name?"

"You're missing my point." Or maybe he'd sensed the part she wanted to remain hidden. *Answer, avoid, ask another question.* "People make judgments about the French. They expect we will behave a certain way. How can that be good?"

"Folks judge almost everyone. But we aren't everyone." Jack took a step closer to her and his voice dropped to a husky murmur. "We've agreed to be husband and wife."

His sudden change in manner made her eager and uneasy. "Shouldn't we continue on to the diner?"

"Don't hide who you are from me, Birdie Bell."

"Aren't you hungry?"

"Tell me again why you sold the curtains."

"Because someone wanted it."

"You wanted it as well. You shouldn't have had to give it up."

"I made it out of anger, which is regrettable. I can be hotheaded at times." *Like my brothers.*

"And your dress?"

"The fabric was the closest I could find to something resembling a peregrine. I made it for you. But you didn't mention it."

"Because I was too busy looking at you."

Birdie flushed and couldn't say a word.

He watched her closely. "What did you hope would happen when I saw your dress?"

"That I'd fit in with your family. That I'd impress you."

"You've impressed me greatly."

"But when you first saw me, I did not. Why did you say *no* so vigorously when I told your grandfather my name?"

"I was married before."

"You wrote this in your letter."

"Lorena shared your small size. But you seem completely different."

Gus had used that word to describe Lorena as well. "How was your wife different?"

"One day she just up and disappeared. We searched but never found her. Then earlier this year we hired a pair of trackers recommended by Sheriff Draven."

The word trackers made her stiffen as much as the word pair. Most people used the term bounty hunters. But Lachlan Bravery had always been referred to as a man tracker or fugitive hunter. Lachlan and his wife were now a team of trackers.

"They say Draven collected bounties."

"He still does."

"So, what prevented him from doing your job himself?"

"He was laid up with injuries. He hasn't recovered from them."

She nodded. That explained Draven's limp.

"And Lorena didn't have a bounty attached to her name. She was merely missing." Jack's voice turned hoarse. "Or so we thought."

She forced herself to ask, "Do your trackers have a name?"

"The Braverys."

The confirmation constricted her throat like a hangman's noose. "You've met them?"

"They came to Noelle to deliver their report. A very diligent couple."

Had they told Jack something about her as well? That was a question she couldn't ask. She could only scan his face for a hint of an answer.

Jack stared at the ground, his expression grim. "They found my wife's grave and more. They unearthed why I couldn't locate her. She'd assumed another name."

"Well, if it ain't Bernadette Bellamy," a guttural voice proclaimed.

Her heart raced with disbelief as she spun to face a past that wouldn't leave her in peace.

A pair of dark silhouettes—one tall and lanky, the other somewhat shorter and a whole lot stouter, strode out of the alleyway beside the Golden Nugget. When the saloon's lamplights revealed their faces, the greed glinting in their narrowed eyes made her skin crawl.

"You're mistaken," Jack moved to stand between her and them. "The lady's name is Miss Bell."

The men halted. The taller one straightened his frame to tower over even Jack's lofty height. His companion thrust out his chest and widened his stance. Having puffed themselves up as much as they could, Stretch and Stout fixed their glares on Jack.

He didn't back down.

She couldn't let them hurt him. She tugged his coat sleeve. "We should go." Her voice came out uneven and low, like the croak of a crow.

"Not before these men tell us *their* names and what they're doing here."

If they knew her name, they'd approached her for one thing—her brothers' last heist, the lost shipment of stolen gold.

"Who are you?" Jack's growled question made her cringe until she remembered he was asking the men and not her.

"We work at the mine," Stout snarled back.

Jack snorted. "Unlikely. You aren't familiar, and my business brings me in contact with The Drum's owner and his men."

Stout's glower turned annoyed. "I said we were miners. Not drummers."

"*The Drum* is what the mayor calls his mine." Jack raised a brow in challenge. "If you worked for him, you'd know that. You aren't very good with names."

"But I've a keen eye for women." Stout's gaze raked her. "Still a pretty little thing. You ain't grown an inch."

"You're strangers to me." That wasn't completely true. While she'd never met them, she knew their kind well. They'd hounded her for too many years. "Go away."

"Never was the sociable sort. Always hiding behind your—"

"I don't know you!"

"But you know what we want. Don't you, *Miss Bell?*"

Stout's tall partner finally spoke in a wheezing voice that

reminded her of those who'd spent too much time underground with noxious fumes. "Tell us where to dig."

Thousands of miles away. North of the border. Somewhere along the Cariboo Trail. She knew as much as them. It didn't matter. Now that they'd recognized her, they wouldn't give up.

And neither could she. *Answer. Avoid. Ask another question. Run away.* But only when Jack was out of harm's way.

She pulled harder on his sleeve. "Let's go. I cannot help them. No one ever shared any lessons about digging with me." She didn't ask a question. She didn't want the conversation to continue.

Stout huffed in irritation. "Is that so?"

"My only talent is sewing."

"Then why are you here?" Stretch demanded in his rasping voice.

Stout's gaze skewered her. "A mining town has no call for a sewer."

"You're wrong," Jack snapped. "She's needed here. But out of work miners who accost people in the streets are not. Go try your luck in another town."

"Can't." Stretch coughed, swallowed convulsively and rushed to finish. "Our only prospects are here."

Stout nodded. "We'll stay and see how they pan out."

The desperation darkening their voices snared her attention. She scanned their clothing. Torn in many places with only a couple of crude patches and even those tearing free again. The attire of men who'd lost hope. Until they found her.

"*Stay* away from Miss Bell," Jack said in an unforgiving tone, "or you'll regret it."

A smirk contorted Stout's mouth. "That's mighty big talk for a man who carries no gun and has only one leg."

Jack raised his hands, his fingers balled into fists, ready to strike. Birdie seized his arm and held on tight.

He froze under her touch. When he finally spoke, his tone was as rigid as his posture. "I may be missing a leg, but I have my wits and friends with the same. If you've been in town long enough to hear about me, someone will know about you. You've damned yourselves."

Stretch glanced over his shoulder as if his past had caught up with him as well. He grabbed Stout by the collar and yanked him into the shadows from which they'd come.

Birdie released her hold on Jack and set off swiftly down the street. He caught up with her in a few strides, took her hand in his, and matched her pace. Her fingers clung to his, safe and content in his large but gentle grasp. But her gaze knew better.

They both kept their heads angled to see if the men followed. When she stumbled in the snow, Jack slowed down and forced her to do the same.

"Are you all right?"

"Just a little tired." A grand understatement. *C'est la vie.* She gave up on looking back and faced forward. It would be a long evening. How many questions would he ask about the miners and her past during their meal at the diner?

"Will you find food at *La Maison*?"

"In their kitchen, *oui.*"

"Then I will take you straight there."

Despite that being for the best, her heart plummeted with disappointment to be parted from him so soon.

He must have sensed her distress because his hand squeezed hers reassuringly. "Don't worry. You'll be safe in a house full of people under Mrs. Walters' spirited defense. But you must keep up your strength. You require food as much as rest."

She doubted if she'd sleep at all tonight. She must rise earlier than ever tomorrow. As soon as Mr. Fulton's store opened, she must claim her snowshoes. She'd traded the curtains for them, and she needed them more than ever now. The snow would be deep where she'd be going.

Non, mais quel désastre! She'd been an *imbécile* to hope she could stop running. Tomorrow she'd not only have to abandon her fabrics and dresses, but this man who'd defended her as strongly as he'd treated her kindly. He deserved better than her.

She would not let her past touch him.

CHAPTER 10

The 3rd day of Christmas
December 27, 1876

"**Y**er courting ain't progressing fast enough." Gus rubbed his arms and stomped his feet to shake off the chill.

Jack kept scanning the street. "She's only been in Noelle two days and three nights." *And already I can't imagine my life without her.*

"Stop pussyfooting around 'n ask her for what you want."

"A lifetime together." Jack's gaze shot to *La Maison* directly across the road from where they stood. He contemplated the upstairs windows trying to imagine which one Birdie slept behind. His heart thudded in anticipation of even a glimpse of her.

"How about," Gus muttered, "starting that life by asking her to move out of that cathouse 'n in with us? Then we won't have to stand out here in the cold again."

"We've only been here a few minutes. And I said you

should go inside and wait in the parlor." He wasn't through scanning the street.

"She can stay in Max's room."

"I don't think that will satisfy anyone." The matchmaker, the railroad, and the town wanted marriages. He wanted only Birdie—as close to him as possible. He still wasn't sure what Birdie wanted.

"To heck with satisfaction." Gus thrust his walking stick in the air like a knight raising his sword. "Birdie's safety comes first. Those miners won't have gone far. Their sort delights in being a thorn in yer side."

So Gus remembered what Jack had told him last night. Lately, he was never certain. This was the first time this morning that either of them had mentioned the two men.

After he'd seen Birdie safely back to *La Maison*, he'd gone in search of them. He'd wanted only to spend more time with Birdie, to keep her close and protect her. But common sense told him he needed to find the miners fast and without Birdie by his side.

He'd visited Draven, scanned his wanted posters, and urged him to make finding the men his top priority. He'd searched the Golden Nugget, the street and alleys, and every business that had been opened. He'd even gone to Hardt's mine and Woody's barn.

He'd questioned everyone he'd found and asked them to come to him immediately if they saw the men or heard anything about them. The few who'd said they sounded familiar had thought they'd left Noelle days ago. He wished that were the case.

He'd collected Gus, taken him home, and opened the trunk with his old rifle from the war. He'd snatched up the firearm but his hand had balked over his father's matching weapon.

Gus had grabbed the gun and made him sit in a chair by the stove. "How many times do I have to tell you—yer not responsible for yer father's death."

"I should've saved him."

"No one tried harder than you to do that."

"How do you know? You were carrying men off the battlefield when the mules bolted."

"I know you. I also know a wagon tipping over is an accident that can't be changed."

Gus had claimed the other chair and they'd commenced cleaning the firearms. As they sat together, he'd told his grandfather everything he'd learned about the miners. Then they'd gone up to their rooms.

Gus probably hadn't slept any more than he had. They'd met downstairs at the same ridiculously early hour. They'd walked outside and down the street, peering in windows and alleys, until they reached *La Maison*.

He'd left the loaded rifles under the counter. He didn't want the miners to discover they'd been mistaken on one point. Surprise was a weapon in itself.

Would Birdie be surprised when she saw him waiting for her? He needed to proceed carefully. He had to get today right. "When you asked Gran to marry you, what did you say?"

A frown puckered Gus' brow. "I don't rightly recall."

"Figures."

"She might have asked me."

"Lucky man."

"Very." Gus grinned. "I do remember saying that I loved her."

Jack hunched his shoulders against a sudden chill from the past. "Saying that to Lorena didn't help."

Gus shook his walking stick at him. "Birdie ain't Lorena."

"No, she most certainly is not." Only two days—and no nights—together and his feelings for Birdie were stronger than anything during his years with and without Lorena. "I vow that before this day is over, I'm going to ask her to marry me."

"Lord love a duck." Gus straightened like a hound on point. "Here she comes."

Birdie stepped out of the *La Maison*. When her gaze found him, she froze with a wide-eyed look—like she might run. Away from him or toward him? He couldn't guess which.

Gus thumped him on the back and knocked him out of his stupor. "Wake up, Sunny Boy. You've got work to do."

CHAPTER 11

*D*oux *Jésus*, why were Jack and Gus waiting outside *La Maison*? Except for the owner of the dry goods store, she'd hoped absolutely no one else would be up at this early an hour.

Gus didn't move while Jack limped across the street toward her.

When he stopped a stride away from her, she blurted, "Are you taking me to Sheriff Draven?"

His brow furrowed. "Do you have need of a lawman?"

"No."

"I'm relieved to hear that. It'd pain my heart to learn you were in trouble. You must tell me though. It's the only way I can protect you."

And who would protect him?

Someone nudged her elbow. Gus now stood close to her as well.

And if something happened to Jack who'd look after his grandfather?

Gus prodded Jack a fair bit harder in his arm. He

gestured with his chin down the street into town. "Yer both moving too slow. Let's go home 'n jabber where it's warm."

Jack held out his hand. She took it without thinking.

A spark lit his eyes followed quickly by the return of his frown. "Your hands are cold as ice. Don't they have a stove in there?" He took hold of her other hand and rubbed them both between his.

Heat raced through her veins. "Not in our rooms upstairs."

"I guarantee you'd never be cold upstairs at Peregrines."

"You have a stove on your second floor?"

"No. But you'd never need one." He raised her hands to his lips and blew warm air on them. "You'd have a mountain of blankets and me."

She swayed toward him.

"Well, I need a stove," Gus muttered. "And I know where to find one. I'll see you two at home. A hot breakfast 'n coffee are calling my name." Gus strode off at a spry pace.

She and Jack followed him immediately, in accord and without comment. Jack didn't let go of her hand. They walked in silence, passed the jail and its sheriff, passed the dry goods store and her snowshoes.

Gus halted by the blacksmith's shop. "I need to get something from Culver."

Jack heaved a sigh. "What happened to wanting to get home?"

"Change of plans for me 'n you. You 'n Birdie need time alone."

"We'll have time when we *all* get home."

"No time like the present. Go on without me."

Jack shook his head. "You know I can't do that."

"Then ask Birdie yer question while you wait for me here. I won't be long." Gus went inside.

His abrupt departure after his puzzling conversation with Jack spiked her worry. "Should we go after him?"

"We'd receive a scolding if we did. Besides, he's safe with Culver. The man's a gentle giant. We first met in the war." He turned to face her. "Birdie, we need to discuss your coming to Noelle."

Her gaze plummeted to the toes of her boots. "You didn't want me to come."

"What? That's not true. Why would you say that?"

"You wrote your letters like a warning."

"I didn't want you to have a hard life."

She shrugged. "Life is seldom easy."

"Easier for some," Jack replied. "My past is a heavy burden."

As is mine.

"I want an honest future, but I've lied to you. I've withheld information about my family because I wanted you to come to Noelle and then—even more—I wanted you to stay. I never did find the items that were misplaced in the office. I suspect Gus has squirreled them away somewhere. And there's Lorena."

Curiosity raised her gaze to meet his. "You said you'd been married in your letters."

"Then I said no more. Lorena is a lie of omission."

"She stole a piece of your serenity, and Gus' as well."

Surprise widened Jack's eyes. "He's spoken of her?"

"Only to say she was different. He mentioned her while talking about your grandmother and parents."

"She *stole* a lot more than my composure."

An ominous chill gripped her.

"I don't think Lorena was ever honest with me. She was a thief."

Her world spun in a dizzying blur. She blinked rapidly and

locked her gaze on the solid structure of the blacksmith shop where Gus had disappeared. "Is that why she—went missing?"

"The Braverys discovered she'd run off with a cardsharp, changed her name, and turned to bank robbery—with her adulterous lover by her side."

"I'm so sorry." *For Lorena and for me. For the hurt I must cause. I must leave you as well.*

"I'm not sorry. Suddenly I'm glad she left."

"That can't be true."

"Actually, I'm more than glad. I'm elated. If she hadn't gone, I'd never have written my letters to you. I'd never have met you. Although you share the same size, you are complete opposites. You are everything I want, Birdie. I had to tell you about Lorena because I didn't want any deceptions between us when I asked you to marry me."

Her heart leapt with hope. When he asked? Was he asking now?

Gus raced out of the smithy. "You won't believe what Culver told me. No one in this town sleeps!"

"Surely some must," Jack replied in a tone as weary as it was amused.

"Culver got married last night to the gypsy woman 'n now he's a father."

"You know fatherhood doesn't happen that fast."

"In this case it can," Birdie said. "Kezia brought her six-month-old daughter to Noelle."

A smile curved Jack's lips. "Well then, Culver's been doubly blessed."

"Yup, and the town received its own blessing. Culver told me what Horatio and Maybelle did."

Jack rubbed the back of his neck. "Hate to ask, but what did they do?"

Gus stared at the sky as if lost in thought. "Dang, can't remember now." He shrugged. "But I'll never forget Culver's most fantastical news!"

Birdie already knew what Gus was about to reveal. A rich Englishwoman named Arabella had arrived yesterday and moved into the cathouse while she visited the mine's assayer, Hugh Montgomery. The haughty woman claimed to be a duchess and had usurped Maybelle's standing as the snob of *La Maison*.

With a broad sweep of his arm, Gus gestured to the town around them. "A tall tale about a lost shipment of stolen gold spread like wildfire last night. They say Sheriff Draven is calling it a fool's gold—lost for more than a decade up in Canada."

Birdie yanked her hand free from Jack's. He reached out to take hold of her again, but stopped short. "Don't run away from me again."

"I must."

"What's going on?" Gus' gaze darted between them. "Didn't you ask her yer question?"

"I told her about Lorena."

"You can't let her leave us. You have to—"

Jack seized his grandfather's shoulder. "We're not rushing Birdie into anything. We all need time to think. Shall we continue our walk to the office where it's warm?" He took a step in that direction, stopped, and waited for her to follow.

When she did, he thrust his hands deep in his pockets and fell into step beside her. Gus stomped ahead of them, stabbing the snow with his walking stick even more irately than before.

"Birdie..." Jack lowered his voice to a whisper. "Whatever's happened in our pasts, today we can begin anew by being honest with each other."

Honesty was a luxury that life had taught her she couldn't afford. "You need a wife who can give you a straightforward future."

"I can't go anywhere without you, nor do I want to. A man's future is not entirely up to him. The woman he wishes to spend the rest of his life with has a say as well."

His words warmed her then made her shiver. With her in his life, would Jack's future be long or short? She wrapped her arms around her waist. "What if I say you don't deserve to be saddled with more sorrow?"

"I can handle anything with the right woman by my side." They strode in unison, their footsteps crunching the snow. He'd once again shortened his longer stride to match hers, but she'd always walked at a brisk pace, so they reached the office all too quickly. "It's a leap of faith. When you're ready, I'll be waiting to jump with you."

CHAPTER 12

*P*erched on a stool behind her end of the counter,
Birdie's gaze kept drifting from her sewing to
the back of the office. What did Jack's carpentry shop look
like on the other side of the wall? What would *he* look like
working there? Sawdust in his hair. Sweat on his brow.
Shirtsleeves rolled up.

He was waiting. She was avoiding.

She wished he'd come out and spend time with her. She
wished she had an excuse to go to him. But not to talk. No
questions and answers. Just them together.

She should be wishing for an excuse to leave the office
and retrieve her snowshoes. Whatever else happened, that
was a must. She owned them, and Mr. Fulton had said to
pick them up any time. But snowshoes were an unusual
purchase. They were meant only for walking—away.

They and their purpose were best kept a secret. She
must hide them at *La Maison*.

A soft knock tapped the front door. So soft that Gus'
head stayed down on the other end of the counter. He
needed to start sleeping at night.

Her gaze darted back to the door. The knock had reminded her of how hesitantly she'd stood outside this office two days ago. Her second knock had been much louder.

That didn't happen today. Silence filled the room.

She hastened to reach the visitor before they grew discouraged and left. When she opened the door, a puff of brisk air spilled in along with a distinctive creak of the wood.

Gus, being well-conditioned to the sensations, woke up and hollered, "Come in. Come in. Get yerselves out of the cold."

Penny Jackson stood on the porch, her eyes wide with surprise. When she rushed to obey, she slipped on her first step.

Birdie grabbed her arm and steadied her while tugging the now blushing woman inside. She shut the door firmly against any escape. "We're going to have to fix that step. Grandpa Gus informed me yesterday it was often slippery. Didn't you, Grandpa?"

"Yes, I did. Tell my grandson. He's the carpenter. We don't want any ladies unwilling to join us because of faulty craftsmanship. Like those windows."

Penny's gaze rose to the glass. "What's wrong with the—? Oh, I see."

"Yes, they're a tad high," Birdie said with a grin, because the height of the windows didn't bother her at present. Not with such a lovely visitor in her grasp.

"I wasn't sure if I should come in," Penny said, "but I couldn't resist seeing all of the fabrics you said where inside the bundles you brought from Denver."

Now that Pearl's amethyst dress was done, Birdie's fingers itched to tackle another special project. Penny's gray eyes and auburn hair would go well with almost anything. *Quelle femme chanceuse!* Penny's groom was lucky as well.

"Do you favor a certain color? Perhaps chiffon or taffeta or maybe a simple gingham? I shouldn't say simple. I can show you a half-dozen patterns to choose from. Tell me what you like."

"Oh, I can't buy anything. I thought I might—"

"*Bien sûr.* Part of the thrill is simply in the looking and the"—she winked—"touching." She drew Penny behind the counter so they stood surrounded by fabrics.

Gus put his head down and was soon snoozing again. She adored the old man but there was nothing like having a woman nearby who might share her obsession...

All too soon, Penny was retreating toward the door. "Thank you for such a warm welcome. I almost forgot my troubles. Unfortunately, I have to go now."

"But you just got here."

Penny laughed. "Birdie, I've been here for at least a half-hour."

"Really? It only seemed like a minute. I hope you'll come back." She bit her lip to stop further words from spilling out. Like how she wanted desperately to stay in town, to remain forever with Jack and Gus, and have Penny for a friend.

"I certainly will be back, soon I hope, and I may need your advice on...on what I should wear as a wedding veil."

Birdie's thoughts raced with ideas. "Earlier this year in Denver, I acquired an exquisite rose-patterned lace from France. We could—" No, *they* could not. She might not be here tomorrow. But she could make Penny's veil this afternoon in case she had to leave tonight. In case? Didn't she mean when?

Jack's suggestion that she take a chance with him was playing havoc with her resolve.

She'd pin a note to the veil with Penny's name and the words "paid in full." That way Penny could pick it up whenever she liked. Right now Birdie had her own item to claim.

"We can discuss the details later." She forced a smile to soften the lie. "Might you be heading into town?"

Penny nodded.

"I'd like to visit a few places. Would you mind if I walked with you?"

"I wouldn't mind at all."

"I must tell Jack I'm stepping out. He's working in his carpentry shop in the back. His grandfather shouldn't be left alone these days."

Penny glanced toward the other end of the counter where Gus slept. "I heard."

No surprise there. Talk spread fast in small towns. The two miners were proof of that. They'd say more if she didn't tell them what they wanted to hear.

What would the town say if she left? Nothing good.

She'd be endangering Noelle's chances to secure twelve marriages and win their railroad line. None of them would want her to stay if they learned about her past. Better for them and her if she left soon.

Mostly best for Jack. Her gaze went to his shop. He'd suffered too much already.

"What's wrong?" Penny's worried eyes scanned her face.

When had she become so poor at hiding her emotions?

She didn't even try to force a smile this time. "I'm concerned about Gus. Will you watch him while I speak to Jack? I won't be but a moment. Still, a lot can go wrong even in that short a time. If Gus wakes, can you distract him if he tries to go outside?"

"I can and I will."

"*Merci.*" Birdie strode down the row dividing the freight

stacks, heading into new territory. She'd wanted to see Jack's carpentry shop and him, and now she would. She paused with her hand raised to knock on the back door. Another moment of hesitation.

Jack had said this was her home. She could go anywhere she pleased. She'd only get one chance to see him in this room. If she couldn't stay with him forever, she'd take every memory she could cram into one last day.

She turned the handle, slipped in, and closed the door behind her.

And stood awestruck. Sweat beaded more than Jack's brow. His arms were bare, but so was his chest. He'd taken off his shirt.

The saw in his hand fell with a dull thud on the nearest surface. Both of his hands were free to hold hers again. Or even better, he could wrap his arms around her and hold all of her.

She gulped for air. Separated from the stove by a wall, this room wasn't even warm. He must have been working extra hard. Laboring with his corded arms, broad chest, rippling abdominal muscles. She gulped for more air. Did he sleep in the nude?

This was definitely an intrusion.

Jack limped quickly toward her. "What's happened? You look flustered." He glanced over her head at the door behind her. "Did someone come in and bother you?"

"Actually, the opposite. A friend visited. She's waiting for me to walk with her into town."

The tension in Jack's body eased. "I'll come with you."

"And Gus?" She tried to keep her gaze on his face, but it kept darting downward. The man had a spectacular physique.

"He can join us."

"Your grandfather is so exhausted he can't keep his head off the counter." And she couldn't keep her eyes off Jack. "Do you realize that you don't have your shirt on?"

"This is why..." He raised his fingers to touch her cheek. "You're blushing." He took a step closer to her. A wince and frown replaced his smile as he rubbed his thigh. "Who's your friend?"

"Penny Jackson. One of the brides."

"Silas' intended," he replied. "The bad luck bride."

"Why do you say that?"

"Gus said people were calling her that in the saloon last night. Being a fellow widower, I'm sympathetic to Mrs. Jackson's loss and her hope for a marriage that lasts. She needs every friend she can get. Are you delivering your other friend's dress?"

"I didn't want to go without telling you."

"What's the hurry? Can't you deliver it tonight? Or even tomorrow?"

"I need to run another errand as well."

"Birdie, you can't outrun your past. You should stay. We can—"

"Is that my future with you? You telling me what I can and cannot do? I'd never stay in a marriage so smothering."

Jack reeled back like she'd struck him.

She reached out to him, but he sidestepped her and limped back to his saw. He yanked his shirt from a nearby wall peg and donned it. "If you've set your mind on leaving, I can't stop you."

"I promise I'll be back as soon as I can."

He shrugged and kept his gaze on the task of buttoning his shirt. "I'll be here. Waiting." His hands paused, but his eyes remained downcast. "Are you going to meet those miners and help them find their stolen gold?"

"No! I'm not a thief. I'm not Lorena."

"You're right. You've shown me that. But you're still leaving."

"Not this afternoon." She winced when she realized the revelation in those words.

He nodded. "It's only a matter of time."

"I don't want to leave. I have to."

"Be careful. Birdie—"

"I'm stronger than I look."

A sad smile curved his lips. "I no longer question that." He squared his shoulders and turned to face her fully. "I wanted to say—Birdie Bell or Bernadette Bellamy, whatever your name, I'll never regret that you joined my life even if only for a few days. Thank you for coming to Noelle." He picked up his saw and resumed his work. "I wish you only happiness and safe travels."

CHAPTER 13

*B*irdie scanned the street as she hurried out of *La Maison*. She sighed with relief not to see the two miners, but also with disappointment for Jack and Gus' absence. She hastened forward. She'd promised Jack that she'd come back. Never had she wanted to keep a promise as much as this.

A few minutes ago at his dry goods store, Mr. Fulton had handed over her snowshoes and wished her a good day. So far so good. She'd left Pearl's dress with a note in their room upstairs, hid her snowshoes in the kitchen downstairs, and now she was free to return to the freight office and Jack.

Her steps quickened. She might be walking alone, but she was headed where her feet wanted to go.

She'd parted ways with Penny outside Mr. Fulton's store when Mrs. Walters had called to them from across the street. The matchmaker wanted to discuss if they were ready to get married. Birdie had commented under her breath that she wasn't up for such a conversation.

Penny had whispered back, "Leave it to me." Then she'd steered the matchmaker away, saying she hadn't seen her groom Silas more than a couple times since the brides arrived.

Silly man. Didn't he see he'd been granted a rare prize in Penny?

Penny, Pearl, and the Peregrines. A smile curved her lips. She had a new-found love for the letter P. And a growing longing for friends, family, and a home. Could it all be possible here in Noelle?

She loved Jack's kindness, his desire to be honest, his strength of body and soul. He knew she might leave him and he'd let her go. She loved him for that as well. Jack Peregrine was a match made in her heart.

Could he love her as well?

She forced her footsteps to slow when she saw the jail. For a small town, this one overflowed with challenges. She hugged the opposite side of the street to avoid walking near Draven's domain in the full light of day.

Any departure from Noelle would best be done in the dead of night. A lantern would be needed to read her father's compass. *La Maison's* kitchen had them and now her snowshoes too. She could leave money for the lantern and some food and slip out the back door. Once under cover of the trees, the lantern could be lit and a course charted around instead of through the town.

With fortitude and feet that didn't sink in the snow, she'd reach the trail she and the other brides had journeyed up. She'd go directly down to the nearest train line—and never see Jack Peregrine again.

Her heart clenched tight. She pushed the parts of her plan to the back of her mind, hiding them like unappealing clothing at the bottom of a trunk. She may need to use them later, but she didn't want to think about them now.

Right now, she was walking toward Jack, not away from him.

She passed the barbershop. Nacho's Diner came next. Jack had always wanted to take her there. Maybe they could try again this evening. He might hold her hand and—

A yank on her hood jerked her sideways off her feet. She struck the ground hard. Couldn't breathe. Saw only the sky. Then a row of grubby fingers. They dragged her by her hood across the cold snow. Two rooftops rose on either side of her. Nothing good ever happened in an alleyway.

She rolled fast. Twisted free. And slammed into a wall of wood. She sat up with her back braced against the side of the diner.

The two miners from yesterday loomed over her.

She dared a glance at the street. She couldn't see the jail. Not counting Nacho's and the barbershop, it was the closest building. *Mon Dieu!* These men were either brazen or stupid to have attacked her so close to Draven's office.

Stout puffed out his chest. "Tell us where your brothers hid their gold."

She hunched her shoulders and wrapped her arms around her waist, trying to act like she was terrified and hurting bad. It didn't take much acting. Under the cover of her arms, she slid her hand inside her coat and found her scissors. "If they had said a word to me about it, I'd have told the first pair of ruffians who dragged me into an alley."

"You're lying," Stout said. "And we ain't leavin' this town without gold in our hands or directions in our heads as to where we can find some."

How long had they been out of work? They'd said they'd been laid off at the mine. If not Noelle's, then another. Or even a string of them. Without a skill like her sewing or Jack's carpentry or Gus' leather tooling, these men were slaves to the lure of a sudden windfall. Not to mention the compulsion to gamble everything to obtain it.

"Tell us." Stout's voice dropped to a growl. "Or we'll make you."

Stretch stayed silent except for his labored, rasping breaths.

"I don't know where their gold is buried. I never did."

"You lived with your brothers in that mining camp."

"Until they started stealing, then they disappeared in the hills."

"Everyone said they still visited you."

She caught herself before she nodded in agreement. They'd been good brothers, just not good men. They'd offered her part of their loot. When she refused to take it, they came back with food. Too hungry to resist, she'd taken it. Then she'd been sick with guilt wondering if it'd been bought with the gold they'd first offered. Gold stained with the blood of the people they'd hurt or killed to acquire it.

She'd taken up her sewing in earnest. Purchased her own food so she could refuse her brothers'. That didn't stop them from seeking her out for stolen moments. A deserted road where they'd hug fiercely. A crowded street with a brief clasp of hands.

"You know more than you're telling us."

She now knew her brothers' visits had fed the rumors that she must be part of their gang or at least knew their hideouts or where they might bury things. If she could go back in time, she'd still have clung to them. The memory of their love had gotten her over many a lonely trail.

"We don't have time for this." Stretch's gaze darted to the ends of the alley. "We gotta go."

"No." Stout raised his fist. "We just need to loosen her tongue."

She met his downward swing with an upward arc of her scissors. Bright red blood ripped across his knuckles. If she'd held a knife, he might not have held onto his fingers.

His flinch of surprise then yelp of pain gave her time to escape his kick. She jumped to her feet and kept her bloody scissors between them. If they wouldn't listen to the truth, it was time to start lying.

"Last night you wondered why I was in Noelle. I couldn't tell you because we were in the presence of an honest man." Every good lie began with some truth.

Stout snorted. "The one-legged freight man."

She fought the urge to cut him again.

"He said you came here to sew. The town says you're here to marry him."

"Do I look like the marrying type?"

Stout's eyes narrowed as he studied her. "You look like a Bellamy. In a high rage. Eyes flashing like blue hellfire."

"And now a Bellamy, when she isn't being accosted on the street, sits in a freight office directly across from a mine."

Stout's eyes widened eagerly. "You're spyin' on them?"

Her heart hurt at how easily he accepted this false and unflattering version of her character, but his reaction told her she was on the right track. She'd finally said something he believed—and liked. She straightened her spine and forced herself to continue. "I'd rather look for stolen gold stashed on the mountain I'm standing on, than on one that's thousands of miles away."

"Didn't know your brothers robbed anything this far south."

"They didn't, but we had friends who did. Unfortunately, they died as well." She fixed her gaze on him and cast her lure. "I'm in need of new partners."

"The Bellamys always liked to build a gang." Envy thickened his voice.

"You joined my brothers?"

"They wouldn't let us."

That said a lot. These men were untrustworthy even by thieves' standards.

"I'd let you. But first I need to maintain my illusion as a bride. My groom expects my prompt return after I run my wifely errands. He's concerned about me walking the streets alone. Imagine that."

Stout laughed. "You're too tiny to do much harm."

Had he already forgotten about the cut on his hand? She didn't remind him. Not when escape and a temporary truce was within her grasp.

"Are you offering to carry all that heavy gold for me?"

"Where's it buried?"

She shrugged. "If I knew, I'd be long gone with the loot. My friends' directions were cryptic." She paused as if trying to recall their exact words. She used the time to concoct something believable that wouldn't endanger Noelle. "*Not in town or at the mine, but nearby on the mountain.*"

Stout's gaze finally left her and swung to his tall friend. "Could it be over behind the mountain by the old—?"

"Shut up," Stretch hissed. "She may talk like a Bellamy, but I've seen how she holds onto her groom and his granddaddy. Like they're already"—his rasping voice turned as envious as Stout's had a moment ago—"family." He pulled Stout away from her and down the alley, only pausing to glare over his shoulder at her and say, "You'd better find the exact location of your stolen gold by tomorrow. Otherwise we'll topple your nest and toss you and your Peregrines into the abyss."

CHAPTER 14

"*Y*er needed elsewhere." Gus' palm slapped the counter. "So why are you still here?"

"I'm not leaving you alone, and Birdie promised she'd come back as soon as she could." Jack kept staring out the office window, looking for her and hoping that *soon* would happen any second.

"You shoulda gone with her."

"Remember the first day she came to see us? She said she'd been on her own since she was sixteen. She doesn't need us to take care of her."

"Don't recall her saying that, but it doesn't matter. It's hogwash. Everyone can use a helping hand."

"Maybe so. But she's on the verge of running away, and we need her to yearn with all her heart to stay with us. That type of longing doesn't involve protection."

"What does it involve?"

"Love and acceptance of every part of who she is."

Gus huffed. "She's Birdie Bell 'n Bernadette Bellamy."

Well, at least Gus remembered a few things.

"It's confusin' as all heck," Gus added.

"Agreed. But Birdie is a puzzle I won't shy away from solving." A grim smile twisted his lips. He'd buried himself in work to avoid learning about his first wife. Not this time. "We dig for the truth and use it to keep Birdie safe. When you were gathering gossip in the saloon and from Culver at the smithy, did it sound like the town had made the connection?"

"Can't remember, but I don't care if they do. We're keeping her."

"Only if she decides to keep us."

"Listen, you need to take her to yer bed."

Jack groaned. "Gus, this isn't the time to—"

Gus thumped the counter again. "You call me Grandpa or nothing at all. And you *listen* to me, Sunny Boy. You need to show that gal what's left of yer leg 'n stop waiting 'n worrying if she'll reject you because of it. You need acceptance too. No more doing things half-measure. Show Birdie yer pain 'n give her the chance to *show you* she ain't Lorena."

The thought of baring himself entirely to Birdie terrified him, but not as much as never seeing her again.

A tiny woman dressed in a long dark coat ran over the bridge and up the rise toward the office. The joy thundering in his heart at the sight of Birdie turned to fear. Something red flashed in her hand.

He yanked open the door.

She sprinted the final strides to reach him.

"What happened?"

Her small palm slammed flat against his chest, struggling to push him back inside. He retreated only to take her in with him. When he closed the door behind them, she braced her back against it. Her palm stayed on his chest. Her other hand hung by her side, clutching her scissors and dripping blood.

"Whose blood is that?" The thought that it might be hers made him light-headed.

Her face went white as the snow outside. "I'm not a killer or a thief."

"I know." He cradled her face between his hands. "You have a kind heart. You give dresses away. Tell me if you're hurt."

Gus appeared beside them. "I can wrap you in bandages till we get you to Doc Deane."

Jack gave him a thankful glance. "Yes. Grandpa assisted the surgeons in the war. We can—"

Her scissors hit the floor with a clatter as she dropped them. She surged forward to wrap her arms around his waist and hug him close. "They didn't hurt me, but I—" She hid her face against his chest. "I cut the stout miner's hand after he and his tall friend dragged me into an alley. I can't make them go away. I can't tell them where my brothers buried their gold. I don't know."

"I believe you."

"But they don't, and now they've threatened to hurt you as well." Her grip on him tightened. "Take me to Draven. Make him haul me away so no one has a reason to come here and harm you and your grandfather."

"Running away isn't the answer."

"It's not running. I'm giving myself up to the authorities."

"Draven isn't taking you anywhere. I won't let him."

"Jack, please listen. I'm not the person you think I am."

"Then tell me who you are—but later, when we have time. Right now, I need a favor."

She lifted her head to gaze up at him. Tears glistened in her dark blue eyes but she raised her chin valiantly.

"I need you to stay with Gus while I ask Draven and the mayor to help me find those men again."

"*Non!* You could get hurt."

"With Draven by my side? I don't think so. I need to find those miners so they'll never threaten you again."

"And you and Gus."

"And everyone else in Noelle. We're saving it from all threats. This is our home."

She shook her head. "I won't be welcome here when the town learns who I truly am. Honest folk can't afford to have a woman with a history of thievery in their midst."

"What I can't afford is to lose you. I don't believe the town will reject you, but if it does it's not a place I want to stay in. We'll leave together."

"You ain't leaving without me," Gus growled. "We're a family. We stick together." Gus patted Birdie's hand reassuringly. "Now don't worry. Just tell us how you escaped those miners."

"I told them there was stolen gold stashed outside of town. I didn't say where, but they said something odd, like they knew where to look and then they left. I couldn't think of another way to escape them."

"Cunning as a fox, you are!" Gus declared. "I couldn't ask for a finer granddaughter."

"But I lied."

Gus shook his finger at her. "You did what you must to come back to us."

"And also made my job easier." Jack stared deeply into her eyes. "What was the odd part about where they might search?"

Birdie sealed her lips and gave him a mulish look.

"I'm going after them no matter what you say or don't say. Will you send me out blind?"

She huffed, then shook her head and raised her gaze to the ceiling as if trying to remember precisely. "Over behind the mountain by the old..." She waved her hands in the air. "After that the conversation halted abruptly and they departed."

"The only thing old on the other side of mountain is the abandoned mine." He kissed her forehead and hugged her close. "I'll find them, Birdie. I promise they'll never bother you again."

But when her arms looped around him and hugged him back just as fiercely, he couldn't move. If he broke their embrace, would he ever get a chance to hold her this close again?

"Don't dillydally." Gus nudged his elbow. "Get going. The sooner you catch those men, the sooner you can get back. Then you two can seek out a bed 'n—"

"Get some rest. It's been a challenging day and it's not over." He released Birdie reluctantly and went behind the counter. This time he didn't hesitate when he reached for the rifles. He pulled them both out. One for Birdie and one for him. "Do you know how to shoot?"

She scanned the firearms curiously, studying them in a way that was uniquely her. "It's been a while. Those are old weapons. Are they from the war?"

"Yes. This one was my father's." He handed the rifle to her. "Now it's yours. Keep it with you at all times. Will you stay with Gus until I return?"

"I promise on all that I hold holy, but only if you promise to come back as soon as you can."

"I will, but I could be out late." *And even if I'm not, I don't want you going back to La Maison.* "It'd be best if you stayed the night."

"Finally," Gus crowed. "Yer listening to my advice. She can sleep in yer—"

"In my brother's room."

Gus scowled at him, then grinned slyly. "She'll require a nightgown."

Jack's vision filled only with the image of Birdie in a thin linen shift. Without the layers of skirts and petticoats, she'd be even tinier. Even with his missing leg, he could easily lift her in his arms and—

"I'm a seamstress. Making the necessary clothing won't be difficult. But first"—her gaze locked with his—"will you agree to do something else for me?"

"You need only ask." *Ask me to take you to the reverend, to carry you to my bed, to hold you all night long.*

"When you've completed your search, I want you to tell Draven my real name."

"There's no reason to—"

"He can protect you."

"And you as well."

"That is up to him. Do we have an agreement?"

"Only if we tell Draven together. I want to go forward with you by my side." And if Birdie wanted that as well, he'd never leave her.

But Draven was a hard man. He'd have his say. Jack would have his as well. He wasn't letting Draven or any man take Birdie away from him. Only Birdie could take herself away from him.

CHAPTER 15

A gust of frigid air, rasping like a saw in a forest, ripped Penny's veil out of Birdie's hand. Like a white flag, it fluttered out of reach above her. Jack caught it and drew it down to her. The wind rose again, grumbling and grinding, whipping Jack's tawny lion's mane around the determined planes of his face.

She leapt to grab hold of him. An invisible force flung him heavenward. She grasped only cold air.

The low flame of a lantern threw the shadow of her outstretched arm over the bedroom door. Her hand dropped to clutch the blankets covering her legs. She drew them up to her chin and curled into a shivering ball on the mattress where she'd fallen asleep waiting for Jack's return.

The bridal veil, now sewn and ready to wear, remained downstairs with Penny's name on a note. The gift might as well have flown away. She'd never see Penny wear it. Other than Denver, she'd never remained long enough in one place to see her creations worn on any day, let alone a wedding day.

If she were lucky enough to marry, she wouldn't care what she wore as long as Jack stood by her side.

Where was he? Why hadn't he come home?

The grating sound that'd tormented her dreams rose again. Not from above but below. Jack had shown her how to bar the front and rear doors with a plank as sturdy as it was heavy. It'd take a saw or an axe to break in.

She couldn't allow any intruders to corner her upstairs.

She leapt out of bed. The icy air made her gasp. Donning her coat over the nightgown muted her shivers. She didn't pause to button it up. She put her mother's scissors in her pocket, grabbed Jack's father's rifle, and opened the bedroom door so slowly it had no chance to creak.

Even though she had only one direction to go—a few strides down the hall to the stairs—her hand went to her father's compass on the chain around her neck.

Oh Papa, you would've approved of Jack.

She had trouble believing Jack's father would've been as accepting of her. But if the man shared any similarities with Jack and Gus, he might have proved her wrong. While standing outside the dry good store, Gus had mentioned his son's name very briefly while dwelling on the women who'd graced his life.

Neither Gus or Jack spoke openly about George Peregrine. Why?

The grating sound stopped. Was that good or bad?

Even wearing a pair of woolen socks, her feet complained with every step on the chilly floorboards. She should've worn her boots, but they'd make too much noise. *Nom de Dieu*, she wasn't thinking straight! She should've hung them by their laces over her arm. Without them, she wouldn't get far outside in the snow.

Zut de zut! She still wasn't thinking straight. She'd

promised she wouldn't leave Jack's grandfather unprotected. No running tonight. Time to make a stand.

A light glowed ahead. The intruders were inside. She raised the rifle to her shoulder. At the end of the hall, she chanced a peek down the stairs and into the carpentry shop.

The silhouette of a tall man with wild hair stood at the bottom step. The same man who'd opened his front door to her on Christmas Day.

"Jack. You're home!" She set her rifle against the wall and raced down the stairs. "How did you get in?"

"Gus let me in."

A fine protector she was. "Why didn't I hear?"

"He said you were asleep." When his gaze traveled over her, a wave of heat replaced the cold. "We have a system. A snowball, or several, thrown against his bedroom wall."

"I heard a noise as well." She glanced around his shop. A lantern lit the main worktable, but consigned the corners to shadows. They were alone.

"I'm sorry I woke you. I was building more shelves for your fabrics."

She felt her eyebrows rise in surprise as her gaze came back to him. "At this hour?"

"I couldn't sleep." He shifted his stance and grimaced. "My body aches from tramping around in the cold."

"Did you find the miners?"

"No, but everyone I asked readily joined the search. Well, everyone except Percy. He objected and called it foolish. We all ignored him." Jack grinned. "See? The town helped you instead of listening to a long-time resident."

"Why?"

He frowned. "Because we take threats seriously and... We have good taste?"

She couldn't help but chuckle. "I meant, why is this Percy fellow so different?"

Jack shrugged. "He has a reputation for wanting to be in charge. The search wasn't his idea. Neither were the brides, but he talks like the plan originated with him now. Could be Percy acts only to impress his uncle who's a member of the railroad board."

"Did you talk to Draven about me?"

He shook his head. "I said I wouldn't do that without you by my side. And it's too late to visit him tonight. You need your sleep. Go upstairs. I'll keep watch down here while I work. In the morning, we'll—"

"*Non.*" Tomorrow would come too soon and then she and Jack would go tell Draven her real name. After that she'd have no guarantee she'd see Jack again. She didn't want tonight—and being alone with Jack—to end. She gestured toward his worktable. "May I see your creation?"

"It's far from finished." He led the way with a limp more pronounced than any she'd seen.

She followed closely, her hands longing to comfort him. Instead, she ran her fingers over the fresh cut wood. Her shelves half-formed. Another gift for her. "It's lovely." Her hands drifted to his tools, some still warm from his exertions. She kept moving, studying by touch and sight his woodwork in varying stages of completion around the room.

Jack followed her silently, holding the lantern high to light her way, until she stopped in a corner where wooden legs hung from hooks on the ceiling.

"Not a pretty sight." His grim tone made her halt a hand's-breadth from the closest one.

"Why do you say that?" She pressed her palm over her heart, trying to calm her rush of anxiety. "You've made them perfectly. They're—"

"Necessary."

Indignation for his creations made her spin to face him. "*Oui, et belles aussi*. Very beautiful."

"You'd feel differently if you saw—" His entire body stiffened. "You should go upstairs."

"So should you."

A muscle jumped in his clenched jaw. "Too many memories hound me tonight."

"Lorena."

"Her memory has shrunk to a cautionary tale. A whisper of what not to do."

"And your father? You and Gus never speak of him."

"Because of my—" Jack rubbed his thigh as he leaned heavily against the nearest wall. "He died in the war."

"The one between the States? Even north of the border the talk of it was endless. A terrible loss for both the south and north."

"Too many died. And not only from gunfire." He stared at the wooden legs hanging beside them.

"Will you tell me what happened?"

"A cannon blast spooked our mules." A flash of pain pinched his brow. The torment assaulted his countenance again and again, like explosions from his past. Until his agony remained deeply ingrained on his face. He spoke haltingly as he continued. "They—bolted down a ravine. The transport wagon tipped over. Trapped my father beneath. I crawled under. One wheel was on his back, slowly squeezing the life out of him. I wasn't strong enough to pull him free."

She stepped as close as she could without touching him. "I'm so sorry, Jack." When he didn't retreat, she raised her hand and gently caressed the haggard lines on his face.

His hand covered hers and pressed her palm to his

cheek. "All I could do was hold onto him." A shudder shook him. "Until the wagon shifted and rolled again. It crushed my leg. I woke up in a field tent the next day. Gus told me he tried to stop them."

A chill skittered up her spine. "Them?"

"The doctors. They cut off my leg. I knew they would. With so many injured, they only had time to save officers' limbs."

Tears blurred her eyes. "Life is cruel."

"I'd have given mine gladly, if I could've saved my father. He wasn't the easiest man to be around after my mother died. But he always put his family's well-being above his. When Max and I joined the war, he didn't say a word. He just went with us."

"And Grandpa too."

A smile tugged his lips. "He's the toughest of us all." Pride deepened his voice. "He and Max used their bare hands to dig me out from under the wagon."

"I'd like to meet your brother."

Jack's smile vanished. "He won't come back to Noelle. He said my need to keep our family together was smothering him."

She cringed. "I'm sorry I used that word."

The warm kiss he pressed against her palm made her toes curl in delight. "I asked for honesty and you gave it to me. You spoke the truth. Lorena said the same. Many times. But she waited years before she left."

"Sounds like she never opened her eyes to see what she was missing."

"She said she missed our carefree youth. We were childhood sweethearts. She honored her pledge and waited for me to come home from the war. When I explained how I'd lost my leg, she still agreed to marry me. Then she saw my stump and accused me of dishonesty."

"But you told her!"

"Sometimes words are not enough. I should've shown her. Instead, I rushed her to the altar. We hurried everything after that. We never lingered over any intimacy, and she refused to sleep in a bed with me. Said she didn't want my half leg touching her."

"You are well rid of her." As soon as she spat out the words, guilt pricked her.

"You look like you've bit into a sour apple. When I first saw you in *La Maison*, you held me captive with the way you studied the room, and then me, so intently. I felt the same as I followed you around my workshop. I'm always wondering where your thoughts are leading you."

"I've concluded it's disrespectful to speak harshly of the dead, but I've never felt more strongly about something I've said. You deserve better, Jack." *Better than Lorena and better than me.*

He shrugged. "And now all I have is Gus."

"Your brother will come back to you, in time. And tonight, we have each other." She glanced toward the door leading to the office. "I'll fetch a dress and work beside you."

He released her hand and retreated a step. His breath hissed between his teeth.

Her gaze went to his leg. "You said your body hurt from walking in the cold. You meant your leg, *oui?*"

"It gives many pains. Some are like phantoms. Memories of before and during its loss. I must have been half-awake. Burying myself in the physical distraction of labor is the only thing that gets me through the days and nights."

"My sewing helps when I miss my family. We are well matched in this."

"But we cannot hide behind our work forever." He raised his hand. It was his turn to touch her face. He didn't stop there. His fingers caressed her hair from the roots to the ends that fell unbound to her waist. "Your hair is as soft as your skin. Softer than any of your fabrics. I couldn't understand this irresistible lure when I tried to organize your belongings after Gus scattered them around our office. Then you knocked on my door and walked into my life."

"The silk, the chiffon, the velvet," she whispered. "Everyone enjoys touching them."

"They hold no allure without you. Being near you has become as vital as breathing. I feared it'd be thus." His fingers slipped through her hair to cradle the back of her head. He pulled her closer. "I cannot stop touching you."

His eyes glowed like molten gold as he lowered his mouth to hers. She closed her eyes and let herself fall into his all-encompassing warmth. His kiss was hot and persuasive. He stole her breath and her heart.

She'd never been happier for a theft. She grasped the front of his shirt as her world shifted with her surrender. This man was her home.

He wrapped his arm around her and held her steady. His mouth left hers to whisper in her ear. "I'm rushing you into this."

"You won't hear me complaining."

"What if you have regrets in the morning?"

"I will not, but I suspect I cannot convince you with words. I need to show you. Will you walk with me upstairs?"

CHAPTER 16

*B*irdie held tight to his hand as she led him up the stairs. She had a solid grip for a woman with such small fingers. His hand engulfed hers and even a step above him he could still look over her dazzling crown of raven hair.

A light shone from the open door of his bedroom. His heart missed a beat. "Did you sleep in my—?" His question was answered when she halted in the doorway.

She'd made a wonderful mess of his bedcovers. The faint depression where her round bottom had rested made his mouth turn dry.

"You said I should sleep in your brother's empty room, but I—" Her fingers tightened around his. "Grandpa said the choice was mine."

"He's right. In our home, you're free to go wherever you wish." He swallowed roughly. She was free to leave him. "What did you want to show me?"

She tugged on his hand, but he couldn't move. When her fingers released his, he let her go, and she pointed to her dress draped over the chair by his bed. "Will you fetch my clothing for me?"

He strove to mute his limp as he walked directly in her line of vision. As soon as he scooped up the dress, he froze once again. The fabric was soft and silky, but his life felt hard and bleak without her hand in his.

The door clicked shut behind him, and his heart started racing like a wagon barreling downhill with no brakes.

"You said you'd keep me warm if ever I slept at Peregrines. When I woke without you near, I was very cold." She pulled her dress from his hands and tossed it back onto the chair.

"What are you doing?" His calves hit the bed as he tried not to brush up against her in the cramped room. If he touched her again, he couldn't guarantee he'd have the strength not to pull her down on the bed with him. "I thought you wanted—"

"Only to get you inside this room." She raised her chin and held his gaze without blinking. "Take off your trousers, Jack Peregrine, and let me show you who I truly am."

He clutched the bed's headboard to steady himself. He couldn't have heard her right.

She watched him with her familiar unreadable expression and tilted head. "Do you trust me?"

"Yes, of course."

"But you still hesitate. I understand. To remove one's clothing is a final act of trust." She gave him an impish smile. "It is difficult to run away when nude. Very conspicuous and cold." Something flickered in her eyes that made him think she was remembering a time that was far from humorous, but she held on to her smile.

"What are you thinking?"

She shrugged one shoulder. "I have my own phantoms."

"Will you share them with me?"

Her gaze locked on his bed. "Two years after I fled the Cariboo gold fields, I fell to a youthful temptation of the heart. Before I could consummate my mistake, I learned my suitor craved more than me. He took the clothes I had willingly removed and my sewing chatelaine which I carried even then. Next, he collected the bedsheets, the curtains, and any scrap of fabric in the room. He left and locked the door behind him."

He squeezed the headboard so hard the wood creaked. His voice echoed the noise in a curt growl. "What did you do?" If he could've reached across time, he'd have wrung the man's neck.

She wrinkled her nose. "Sadly, I must admit I curled up in a ball of misery. For how long I do not know." A wry smile replaced her grimace. "But then he did me a favor. From his side of the door, he told me I'd remain naked until I gave him a satisfactory answer concerning the location of my brothers' gold. His honesty set me free."

He scowled in displeasure. "For all my cravings for the truth, I'd rather he favored you with the return of your scissors."

Her brows arched as she nodded. "Me too. But all I had was an empty room. I ran my fingers over every surface and crack, searching for a way to escape." She exhaled a relieved-sounding sigh. "And got lucky. A needle must have fallen from my sewing case."

"What could you do with something so small?"

She leaned toward him like a conspirator. "I surprised him. When he opened the door, I was ready. I pricked the sensitive parts of his body."

Jack couldn't help but flinch and cover his groin with his free hand. "He deserved worse."

Her lips parted in surprise. "I meant his ears and neck! He was after all still clothed." A flush stained her pale cheeks. "I finally reclaimed my garments and scissors from the floor outside the door. I didn't stop to dress until I was clear of the town and hidden in some leafy—and therefore lovely—dogwood bushes."

He released the breath he hadn't realized he'd been holding while he surmised the rest of her story. "And you continued running and haven't stopped." She'd run from him on Christmas Day when he'd put his arm out to keep her with him. But she'd come back the next day and every day following. "Why do you stay in Noelle?"

She went very still. "Temptation."

She'd used the word to describe the wretch who'd held her prisoner. *A temptation of the heart.* Anger and hope warred in his. Had her heart been tempted again?

"Did you love him?"

"I thought so, and that he loved me. It was the reason I forgave his many impatiences that resulted in unkind remarks followed by pleas for forgiveness and sympathy. I ignored all the signs that he was digging for more than me."

"I want only you." Despite his declaration, he gripped the headboard tighter. He couldn't risk touching her when they stood so close to his bed.

"I feel the same."

Her words made his chest swell with happiness. "You're tiny but tough. Single-minded but surprising." He grinned. "Like your needle. You never stop showing me that you're my perfect match." His conscience made his gut roll. He wasn't being honest with her. "You're my perfect woman, while I'm not even a whole man."

Fury flashed like lightning in her dark blue eyes. "You wrote that in your letter. Did Lorena say those vile words?"

"Wasn't only her. Every town we came through after the war said the same. Noelle was no different, even after we chose to stay here."

She shook her head so vigorously she sent her dark hair swinging. "I've glimpsed many kind people in this town. I'd wager they'd say differently. And I'm not just speaking of the brides who've recently arrived."

"The hostile voices tend to drown out the rest."

"Like the miners. And Maybelle and Horatio."

"They drove me to master my carpentry, so I could make my wooden legs and stop using my crutches and canes."

"And the world is a better place because of your creations. But what of your world? You hide your leg from everyone, including me. We have circled around to my request for full disclosure. Shall I go first?" She shoved her coat from her shoulders and grabbed the skirt of her nightgown.

He seized her hands to halt her. "Slow down. We shouldn't rush this."

"I think we should. At least the disrobing part. You asked me once to take a leap of faith with you. It is a quick thing, is it not? To leap?"

Hands still clutching hers, he sat down heavily on the bed. She was right. *Do it fast. And first.* He couldn't ask her to jump off a precipice with him. "I need you to stay still for a moment."

She gave him a solemn nod. "I can be still as a bird."

He didn't doubt it. Her unwavering gaze held his as he pulled off his boots and shirt, then unbuttoned his trousers. When he went to drag them down, he suddenly became all thumbs. Cloth tangled and trapped. He dropped his gaze to find the holdups and shed his last defense. Over his knees and ankles and onto the floor with the rest.

He couldn't lift his gaze. He stared at her small feet bundled in socks below the hem of her nightgown. She stood steadfast while he trembled like a stubborn-fool mule who'd slipped his harness but was too bewildered to do much else.

He sat naked before her, bared completely to her gaze.

"Are you ready?" Her hushed voice filled the room and him with longing. "Am I free to move now?"

"Yes." His reply was little better than a rasp of sandpaper. He might never be ready, but he wanted her to be free.

She dropped to her knees in front of him. Her darkly enticing hair came in line of his vision, but not her eyes. She kept her gaze down, lashes lowered, and slowly, as if she sensed his turmoil, laid her palms on his knees.

One of flesh and bone. The other of wood and hinges.

He relaxed into her gentle touch then tensed with desire. No hiding that from her either.

"Your legs are beautiful. Both of them." Her fingers moved to the straps binding him to the wood. "Will you show me how to undo these?"

He did. And she touched everything she couldn't reach before, without hesitation. But her gaze remained lowered and her mood once again hidden.

"What are you thinking?" He couldn't stop asking that question.

"That you have very warm skin." Her voice had dropped to a throaty murmur that made his blood burn even hotter. "A fire resides inside you. I crave your warmth."

"From the moment I saw you studying *La Maison's* front hall so intently you brought a thaw to my cold heart. I couldn't believe that you were smiling."

"It was an intriguing situation."

"Then you looked at me. And you didn't smile again until you saw my limp."

"I was happy to have finally found my groom."

"Now you find yourself in my bedroom. Seeing all of me. But you do not smile or meet my gaze."

"Because I become selfish whenever you are near." She jerked her hands away from him and crossed her arms like a shield over her chest. "I want what I fear I can never have."

"You have a permanent place in my home and my heart."

Her shoulders slumped. "And what about a place by your side? Not only in your office but in your bed. Every day and night. All night long. No half-life."

Her words reminded him of Gus'. *No more doing things half-measure.* "We cannot do that without..." He hauled in a deep breath. "Will you marry me first thing tomorrow, as soon as we get out of bed?"

Her gaze shot up to meet his. Her blue eyes danced with a light so bright and lively she made him dizzy with hope. "Finally," she whispered, "you've asked."

He raised his hand but stopped a hairsbreadth away from touching her. "And your answer is?"

"*Oui!* Yes!" She flung her arms around his neck. "You are my home, my liberation, my love."

"My love." He echoed her words with a whoop as he scooped her up in his arms so he could turn on his seat and lay her on the mattress.

"*Mon univers.*" Her fingers tangled in his hair and tugged him down with her.

"What does that mean?" He stretched out beside her and let their legs intertwine as well.

She did not pull away or even flinch. Instead, she snuggled closer. "My everything."

"How did I get this lucky? God bless Noelle for bringing you to me." He ran his fingers over her back, the arc of her neck, and the line of her jaw. He only stopped when he touched the blossoming curve of her lips. "Let me show how much you mean to me, *mon univers*."

She kept smiling as he kissed her while she wiggled out of her own clothing and threw it on the floor beside his. They kept each other warm all night.

CHAPTER 17

The 4th day of Christmas
December 28, 1876

*B*irdie couldn't stop touching Jack as they left their
bedroom and came down the stairs, heading for
the freight office. He seemed like-minded, but since he held
her hand and a lantern, he could only use his lips and his
gaze to express his affection. But he used them well.

His golden-brown eyes glowed like sunbursts amid a
shower of slow and fast kisses that kept caressing the top of
her head and several shiver worthy spots on her neck.

Her pulse raced even faster when he bent to whisper
close to her ear. "I can't wait to get you home and complete
what we began. And then start all over again."

She couldn't wait either. She didn't *want* to wait. But
she'd given up telling Jack that.

They'd kept each other blazing hot all night long, but
they had not consummated their union. Jack had insisted
that he wanted to call her Mrs. Peregrine when he took that
particular leap with her. She'd discovered her husband-to-

be, whom she'd previously come to believe was the most patient and giving man she'd met, held an unbendable stubborn streak on certain matters.

But so did she. She didn't pause to look at anything in his carpentry shop today. She pulled Jack through the room as fast as she could and yanked open the door separating them from the freight office. "Hurry! Let's collect Gus and go to the Golden Nugget."

"What's the all-fired rush?" Gus grumbled in a sleep-roughened voice as he popped up from his usual spot where he'd been sleeping with his head on the counter. "Isn't it a tad early to be heading to the saloon for a drink? And who the heck is calling me Gus?"

"*Pardon, Grand-père.* I mean, Grandpa. I'm too excited to speak properly."

"If *Grand-père* means Grandpa, I'm all for calling me that instead. Makes me sound fancy." Gus rubbed his eyes as he watched them hasten up the row dividing the storage area. When his gaze found their clasped hands, he slapped his knee and gave them a grin so wide it made her want to do a jig.

Jack set his lantern on the counter well clear of Gus' end —which was covered in bits of leather—and twirled her by her hand, like he shared her desire to dance. The single turn halted with her standing with her back to him. He grabbed her other hand and, folding his arms over hers, hugged her close with her spine snug against his chest.

Gus' bushy brows arched in wonder and then he whooped. "Glad to see my Sunny Boy shining so bright! I'd hoped you two had a good reason for sleeping in this morning." He yawned. "Me. I've been up for hours."

Birdie wondered if dozing at the counter counted as being up. She didn't have time to ask. She wanted to get married. Fast. "Grandpa— I mean, *Grand-père!* We have joyful news."

"Did you hear that Woody 'n his bride got married yesterday?"

Birdie gasped in delight. "That's wonderful."

"It surely is," Jack added. "However, that isn't our news. We—"

"I know. I was worried too. His wife—" Gus scratched his beard. "Ain't that a kick in the noggin'. I knew her name a second ago, but now I can't remember."

"It's Meizhen," Birdie said. "But we—"

Gus snapped his fingers. "Right. Meizhen almost left town, but then she realized what *we've* known for a long time."

Birdie couldn't stifle her sigh of impatience.

Jack's breath tickled the top of her head as he chuckled. When the sound vibrated from his chest to her back, she sighed for an entirely different reason.

"No use rushing a good story," he murmured against her ear.

She leaned back and let her head rest against his shoulder as she decided it wasn't a hardship to stay exactly where she was and allow her marriage to happen when the world was ready. "What have we known for a long time, *Grand-père?*"

"That Woody is one-of-a-kind," Gus replied without hesitation. "A diamond in the rough."

"And his new wife has exactly the right polish and poise to make their future perfect." She squeezed Jack's hands. "Meizhen and Woody are another case of certain opposites harmonizing. As are Felicity and Reverend Hammond. My head still spins when I recall how swiftly they married. And Kezia and Culver as well."

Jack raised one of their clasped hands and planted a kiss as reverent as it was scintillating on her wrist. "And now it's our turn. But we could use more witnesses. Grandpa, were Woody and Meizhen heading into town or to the barn?"

"How should I know?" Gus rolled his eyes. "I haven't talked to Woody in days."

Birdie stiffened at the same time that Jack did.

She watched Gus closely as she asked, "If he or Meizhen didn't stop by this morning, how did you hear they got married?"

"Did you leave home alone again?" Jack's tone had gone gruff with worry.

Gus scowled at them. "Are you two teamin' up against me?"

"*Non, Grand-père.* Never."

"We're just concerned."

"Well," Gus huffed. "I can truthfully tell you I've been sitting here for hours working on my leather tooling. I had no visitors. Nor did I visit Doc Deane like I done the other morning, but..." Gus stared at the door as if suddenly confused or distracted.

"But?" she prompted

"Doc has news as well. He aided a mother in birth. Her name is another I'm struggling to recall." He tapped the counter impatiently. "Might've been Fay."

"Grandpa," Jack groaned. "No woman by that name lives in Noelle."

"It'll come clear later. Right now, I've remembered some-thing else." Gus rummaged through the debris on the counter before turning back to them. "Congratulations!" Cupped in his hands lay a leather case stamped with a tiny but round bird on a branch surrounded by a forest of leaves. "I made you a wedding present."

"*Oh, Grand-père, comme c'est beau!* I couldn't have asked for a more magnificent gift. Thank you."

Gus flushed with pride. "I hoped you'd like the bird."

"*Mais bien sûr!* I do."

"So do I." Jack chuckled. "She's a plump little thing."

Birdie twisted around to look up at him. "How do you know it's a she?"

"Because she reminds me of you."

She felt her eyebrows rise. "I'm plump?"

He pressed his palm over her stomach. "With luck, one day you will be."

The easy intimacy of his touch made her smile as she imagined holding a baby with Jack's golden hair and eyes.

"You haven't seen everything." Gus flipped over the case and pointed to two loops on the back. "I added these so you can carry it on yer sewing belt."

She immediately reached to add it to her chatelaine. "It's heavier than it appears."

"That's cause there's more to the gift inside. Take a look," he urged.

When she did, she found a jackknife, a tin of matches, a brass whistle, a bandage roll and ointment, and a small flask made of finely worked silver. Her gaze darted up to search Gus'. "*Grand-père*, what is this?"

"It's a survival toolkit."

Jack heaved a sigh as he leaned against the counter. "Not counting the flask, it's the items that went missing from the Christmas Eve shipment."

"Nothing's missing," Gus objected. "It's all here. And so are we, but—" He halted abruptly and cleared his throat. "If you ever got lost, this will help you stay safe till you find yer way back to us."

A sudden wetness in her eyes was mirrored in Gus' and Jack's. "I love my gift more than ever. All of it."

"The flask," Jack muttered in a gravelly voice, "looks like Culver's silversmith work."

Gus nodded vigorously. "I got it yesterday when I visited him."

"Did you—?" Jack sealed his lips and shook his head.

She knew what he'd been about to ask. Had Gus taken the flask without Culver knowing?

Jack opened and closed his mouth several times as if struggling to find a less accusatory way to ask. "How...much did you pay for it?"

Gus threw his hands in the air. "Have you completely mislaid yer manners? That's a terrible thing to ask about a gift 'n I wouldn't tell you even if I remembered. But I can say that everyone, be they man or woman, can use a drop of whiskey for cleaning a wound or fortifying their heart. And that's why I chose the flask."

She kissed his cheek and attached the case to her belt. "You, *Grand-père,* are very wise. A bride never received a finer wedding present. I shall wear it with pride."

Gus gave Jack an I-told-you-I-know-what's-best look, but the instant he turned his back to tidy his end of the counter, Birdie emptied the contents of the survival case into a cloth, folded it up tight and handed it to Jack.

"You must give these to their rightful owners immediately," she whispered.

Jack lowered his voice to match hers. "And then I'll *immediately* buy them back and return them to you."

"Or we can wait to order more. There's no rush. I'm not going anywhere."

Jack glanced from the loot in his hand to the door to her.

"I'm not happy about *going anywhere* without you by my side."

"Someone should stay with Gus."

"We could take him with us." His shoulders sagged, realizing no doubt how Gus' love for conversing would complicate his current task. "We could wait and return these later."

"A delay might open the door for more woes. I do not wish to get married while in the possession of pilfered goods."

He exhaled a resigned breath and raised his voice to its usual volume. "Grandpa, I have an errand to run, but when I return, be ready to go to the Nugget."

"What in tarnation would take us to the saloon this early?" Gus asked. "I can't imagine why you need a drink this bad."

She grabbed Jack's coat from the peg by the door and held it out to him. "Hurry up, Jack Peregrine. The sooner you leave, the sooner you come back."

He donned the coat, but then wrapped his arms around her. "I promise I'll be back as soon as I can."

She hugged him just as tightly. "And I promise I'll be here waiting for you."

He raised his head and scanned her face. "You're done running? You're no longer worried what the town might say or do?"

"They can say whatever they want. They can also throw me in jail or cart me away for questioning in a court in Denver or another country. I'm willing to risk all of that to spend one more second with you—today in our home in Noelle."

CHAPTER 18

*J*ack hadn't been gone more than a minute when the front door flew open with a screech so loud it made Birdie jump. A vulgarly dressed woman strode into the office and slammed the door behind her.

"If you've come to question me about the lady I'm seeing," Gus growled like a wolf guarding his den, "you can turn around 'n leave."

A second jolt of surprise made her study Gus closely. His lips formed a hard line while his eyes shot daggers at their visitor. He appeared too irate to be confused. But seeing a lady? When would Gus have had time for that? There were few occasions where she'd seen him outside Peregrines' Post.

"*Meezeir*, men who obey my rules have *leetle* quarrel with *moi*." Madame Bonheur's fake French accent and arrogance were unmistakable. "My *dezpleasure eez* with your grandson's unwillingness to give me *heez beeznus* as well. Today..." She glanced at Birdie and snapped her fingers. "*Et voilà!* My *dezires* come true."

Birdie planted her palm on her hip, close to the scissors on her belt. *"Espèce de pourriture. Votre français est déplorable."*

The madam blinked in bewilderment. *"Excusez-moi?"*

"Quel est le problème? Was I speaking too fast for you?"

"Nope. Not for me." Gus' guffaws echoed off the ceiling. "I clearly heard you call her deplorable."

"Oui, and a lousy swine. Madame Bonheur, your brash fakery is not welcome here."

The madam glared down her nose at her. "We have not met, but you know my name. My reputation is as large as you are small. And now that your guardian has departed, we shall parlay." She may have dropped her French chicanery, but she continued playing a game similar to a cat taunting a mouse.

This was no random visit. The woman had chosen specifically to wait until Jack left.

Birdie struggled to contain her growing alarm. "Speak as plainly as you can. Why are you here?"

"Let's say I want a dress."

"And if I will not sell you one?"

With an overabundance of hip swaying, Madame Bonheur sauntered up to the counter. "I will convince you to reconsider." On her side farthest from Gus, she drew a derringer from a hidden pocket in her skirt.

Birdie tamped down her shiver of fear. "You expect me to believe you want a dress this badly?"

"You are merely a means to an end," the madam hissed in a low voice. "I want *La Maison* back."

"What are you whispering to my granddaughter?" Gus demanded.

"That I hope she shares my desire to keep my customers healthy. Sadly, older men do not recover so easily from injuries." The madam tapped her derringer against her hip.

She had to get the woman away from Gus. "Shall we discuss your *dress* outside?"

"An excellent idea. Better grab your coat. It's chilly where you're going."

"Birdie ain't going nowhere," Gus protested. "She's staying with us."

Madame Bonheur tsk-tsked. "Such stubbornness is bad for a man's health."

"*Grand-père*," Birdie rushed to say, "do not worry. I'll only be gone a moment." The second she got the madam outside, she'd duck back inside and bar the door against her.

She donned her coat. When the madam opened the door, she fiddled with doing up her buttons, hoping the madam would get impatient and step outside before her. When she didn't budge, Birdie was forced to go first.

She pretended to shiver with cold and apprehension as she folded her arms over her waist—with one hand tucked inside her coat and grasping her scissors. She marshaled her strength to strike fast.

Unfortunately, the madam was faster. She shoved Birdie's shoulder hard and made her stumble. While she regained her balance, Madame Bonheur had closed the door and leaned against it, blocking Birdie from returning to Gus.

The woman waved her miniature gun at Birdie like an admonishing finger. "Love makes idiots of us all, Miss Bellamy."

"How do you know that name?"

"I've learned many things since your arrival in Noelle, while all you've guessed is that I'm not French."

"Your use of my old name tells me you're greedy for gold. You believe I can lead you to a treasure."

"No, I don't. I'm smarter than the pair of addle-headed

miners I found hiding in Felice's room last night. They tried to convince me to let them stay without paying." The madam gestured wildly with her derringer. "When I showed them I wasn't a weak female, they hastened to assure me they'd pay five times Felice's usual fee if I didn't turn them over to Draven or toss them out into the cold. They mentioned a rich prospect and, when pressed, named you as their accomplice. Said your real name was Bernadette Bellamy and you belong to a gang of gold thieves."

"And?"

Madame Bonheur gave her a pitying look. "And you don't want your groom to hear this sordid tale, do you?"

Birdie raised her chin. "He knows. I told him everything about my past."

The madam's eyes narrowed. "I don't believe you. But even if I did, have you forgotten about Draven?"

"Jack and I plan to tell him as well."

"But Jack's not here now. What happens if I take you at gunpoint to Draven and reveal what you've said? The man has a reputation for being cold and heartless. I'd speculate he'd believe you duped Jack into being your accomplice. You're both criminals now."

"Jack's innocent of any wrongdoing!"

"You just revealed he knows about your past but hasn't told the law. You've damned him. And what of his grandfather?"

"What about Gus?"

"I'll only regain *La Maison* if it holds no brides waiting to marry. If you blasted women left town, I'll reclaim all of the men's attention and dollars as well. I'm willing to sacrifice a few men to get what I want."

"If you stoop to murder, you'll draw down Draven's wrath."

"I won't use my derringer. If Augustus Peregrine's care-taker is detained even temporarily, I'll merely turn my back —and order my girls to do the same—if I see the old man doing anything dangerous, like wandering off into the snowy wilderness."

"You're pure evil."

Madame Bonheur pouted as if she was hurt, but her eyes danced with amusement. "How can you be so cruel when I brought you a goodbye gift?" She grabbed some-thing leaning against the side of the freight office and shoved it into Birdie's arms.

She gaped at her snowshoes.

The madam cackled with glee. "I also like to hide things in *La Maison's* kitchens. Luckily, I hid myself before you saw me there yesterday. You bought these so you could leave town, so go!" She made a shooing motion with her hands. "Go now and Jack will remain free to help his grandfather. Stay and we visit Draven and you can beg him to spare Jack."

"I can't leave Gus on his own."

Madame Bonheur held her tiny gun behind her back and waved to a man about Gus' age who was walking over the bridge and up the street toward the office. "Ezra Thorn-ton," she called. "Will you keep old Mr. Peregrine company until his grandson returns? He'll come back shortly, or so Miss Bell assures me."

The man quickened his pace to reach them. As soon as he did, he pinned her with a worried look. "What's wrong?"

Birdie had never met him, but his obvious concern for Gus made her like him instantly. She couldn't allow the madam to hurt either old timer. "Nothing's wrong. I just have to"—she shrugged her shoulder—"go elsewhere."

As soon as Ezra Thornton slipped inside the office, the

madam braced her back against the closed door again and glared at her impatiently. "Are you willing to squander your one opportunity to protect the Peregrines? Hell's gonna break loose if you don't move, or if Jack returns and I have to start shooting in self-defense. Tick tock." She tapped her derringer against the snowshoes that Birdie now clutched with both arms. "Time to strap those contraptions to your feet and flee like they were wings."

CHAPTER 19

The icy cold turned her breaths to ghostly gusts. Sheltered by the trees, the wind couldn't whip away the miniature specters or deliver a warning from beyond. Even the rhythmic pounding from the mine, a noise she'd never had the time to learn more about, had grown muffled. The crisp isolation of the woods did little to ease the internal heat fanned by her exertions.

She'd found her familiar stride. The rhythm of running. Feet lifted and laid precisely, compensating for the width and length of her snowshoes. Eyes focused forward, scanning for the easiest path through the woods running parallel to the main trail—down the mountain and away from everything she'd come to love.

Her enthusiasm for her sewing and fabrics paled next to her affection for Gus and her passion for Jack. Would they ever forgive her for leaving?

She'd never forgive herself. She'd promised to stay, but instead she'd left and ruined an opportunity for Jack to find happiness and for the town to win their rail line.

A faint sound echoed through the treetops, brief and abrupt, and impossible to guess where it'd come from.

She fought the urge to look back. Jack wouldn't be behind her. If he or Draven or anyone else came after her, they'd be on the main trail. She wouldn't see them and they wouldn't see her. Not hidden in these trees. And since they didn't know she had snowshoes, they wouldn't guess to look for her off the trail.

Her escape plan had worked, and would keep working as long as she kept moving forward.

Once again, she traveled light with only the clothes on her back, her father's compass, and her sewing chatelaine with her mother's scissors. The only thing she carried from Noelle was Gus' beautifully engraved but empty survival case and her memories. Three tumultuous days careening between apprehension and happiness. And one gloriously perfect night.

Of all the people who could've finalized her departure—Jack, the sheriff, the miners—a merciless madam had done the deed. A woman whom she had not given a thought after her first day in town.

A break in the forest made her halt. Ahead lay a hollow that'd probably hold a pond come spring. Right now, it was a blindingly white gap in her safe haven.

She held her breath and listened. A lone chickadee sang in a nearby branch. Otherwise her surroundings were silent.

A quick sprint would limit her exposure. But now that she'd stopped, her legs refused to move. She glanced over her shoulder. No gaps there, just trees and snow marked with her tracks leading back to Noelle.

Back to Jack.

She blinked the tears from her eyes and leapt in the opposite direction. Two strides later, a cacophony of shouting erupted on her left. Shock made her stumble and fall on her knees in what she recognized too late was a creek bed that ran straight to the main trail.

Two men jumped from a road of compacted snow. Their exuberance at seeing her dissolved into cursing as they sunk to their knees in the soft deep snow. They floundered toward her, struggling but determined.

She shoved herself onto her snowshoes and sprinted away from them. The familiar sound of Stout's snarl and Stretch's rasp peppered her with commands to halt.

The trees enveloped her like an embrace. She ran until she fell again. Then she crawled behind the nearest tree trunk, braced her back against it, and struggled to hear above the pounding of her pulse.

No footsteps crunched the snow. No shouting or cursing or labored breathing ruffled the air. Even the chickadee had gone mute.

Had Stout and Stretch gone back to the road? If they had, it'd be foolish to hope they'd turned back. They were most likely racing down the trail to find a new spot to ambush her.

How had they found her in the first place? She couldn't believe Madame Bonheur had told them where she'd gone. The madam wanted her to stay gone.

But the woman had mentioned talking to the men last night. Maybe they'd chosen to follow the madam or skulk outside the freight office. Either way, they must've watched Birdie flee with her snowshoes.

She couldn't stop now. She got up and pressed forward. An increasingly uneven stretch of ground slowed her progress. She wound her way around rocks that suddenly rose to form a wall with only one way to go—toward the road.

She froze in dread. Four days ago, the brides had passed through a narrow pass on their way to Noelle. This rock now channeled her toward that spot. If the miners got there before her, they'd lay in wait.

A crunch of snow made her stiffen. A muttered curse had her backing up. Her pursuers weren't waiting. They were using the wall to head straight toward her.

She fled back along the path she'd come. As soon as the wall was low enough, she scrambled on top of it. Her only hope was to use the stone to hide her tracks.

A shout echoed behind her. Footsteps pounded along the rock. Gaining ground. Much too fast. The hard terrain kept the men free from the snow that had previously slowed them down.

She leapt for the largest patch of white she could see and prayed it was deep. It held her weight when she landed and scrambled over it. Two thumps and grunts came close behind her, followed by a crack as loud as a gunshot.

The sound invoked the memory of running from Lachlan Bravery. Fourteen years ago, she'd anticipated a similar retort when she'd glanced back and saw the tracker with his Winchester raised and pointed at her, but he'd never fired his weapon.

This time when she looked back she found Stout and Stretch wading through hip-high snow toward her. The crack came again. The snow beneath her feet shuddered. She fell onto her backside and slid downhill.

The snow went with her in a rumbling wave that soon roared. She dug her snowshoes into the surge only to have them snap like twigs. She flailed her arms in search of something solid to latch onto.

When the avalanche parted from the mountain in a vertical drop, she found only air and screamed.

CHAPTER 20

*J*ack's entire world shook with Birdie's cry. Stripped of its snow, the unforgivingly rigid rock punished his legs equally as he sprinted to the edge where she'd fallen. He slammed to a halt on the precipice, swaying dangerously close to going over as well.

A dizzying drop filled his vision. At the bottom, two bodies sprawled. Limbs twisted at unnatural angles. Unmoving and unreachable. Men rendered small by distance and disaster.

No sign of an even tinier figure. No vibrant flare of a woman's skirt. No rich raven hair across the white. The avalanche had stolen her from him.

"*Jack.*" Her voice calling his name brought him to his knees.

He bowed his head and leaned into the abyss.

"Jack, stop! Don't come any closer."

Below him, a shredded tree dangling by its roots from the rock face came alive with the form of a woman crawling up and out of its mangled branches.

"You're alive!" He dropped flat on his belly and thrust down his hand.

Her eyes shone like sapphires from a face covered in a dusting of snow as she smiled and strained to grab hold of his hand. Unsuccessfully. Their fingertips were twice the length of his arm from touching.

She sat down, grasped the hem of her coat and raised it to reveal her torn skirt. "*Au revoir, mon amie.*" She pulled her scissors from her belt and commenced cutting. "You served me well when you snared this tree and halted my descent, but now I must transform you."

"What're you doing?"

"Making something unique and useful for my current situation." Her scissors flashed as she sliced her skirt into strips and wove them together, with not a shred wasted. She held up a rope.

He caught the end she tossed to him and pulled her up. The instant she was close enough, he looped one arm around her waist and fell back against the stone with her on top of him. "You ran away."

"You came after me."

"I couldn't let you go." He stiffened with dread.

"I know what you're thinking. But if I'm the one stretched out on you, surely it must be the other way around. I'm smothering you." She laid her head on his shoulder and sighed. "I hope you like it because I do."

He forced his muscles to relax as he held her, giving her the chance to wiggle free if she wanted. "Gus told me that Madame Bonheur asked you for a dress."

"She made her request with a derringer in her hand."

"She threatened you?" He clenched his teeth to stop himself from calling the woman the worst of names.

"Not me." She shook her head. "Grandpa Gus."

"He forgot to mention a gun." His surly tone made him roll his eyes as himself.

"She kept it hidden from him."

The madam's brazen behavior made him huff then laugh. "Because she knew it wouldn't stop him. He's not keen on letting you go either. He raised a search party and showed how many people in this town are willing to help you."

"What if it's not enough?" she asked in hushed voice.

"It's enough to convince me once again that we're safer together than on our own. And happier too." He sat up with her in his lap. "Will you come back to Noelle with me and show Gus that you're unharmed? He took it very hard that you disappeared while under his care."

She nodded and hand in hand they walked slowly back along the rock he'd sprinted across moments ago.

"How did you find me so quickly?"

"That's a long story."

"It's a fairly long walk back to town, so I think we have time."

He chuckled. "Well, when Ezra dashed into Peregrines instead of you, Gus was spitting mad. As soon as the two old timers realized you and Madame Bonheur had vanished, they joined forces and roused the townsfolk to look for you. They went to Woody and Meizhen at the barn, and then Mayor Hardt and Hugh Montgomery at the mine and assayer's office. Everyone they met joined them without hesitation."

He scrambled down the rock to the snowy path that would lead them along the ridge to the road. Birdie didn't hesitate when he reached up to lift her down beside him again.

He hugged her close before walking once again with her

hand in his. "They formed a search party that worked its way into town where they found me at Culver's blacksmith shop talking to him and Kezia."

"You returned the flask?"

"I tried." He stopped and put his free hand into his coat pocket. "Culver refused to take it, saying he was happy he'd finally found a way to say thank you for the leather tool-roll Gus made for him but would never take payment for." He pulled the flask from his pocket and held it out for her to take. "It's yours to stow in Gus' survival case."

Birdie gasped and thrust her hand inside her coat, then slumped in relief. "I thought I might have lost his gift in my tumble." She released his hand so she could take the flask and restore it to its rightful place.

His chest tightened with love for the reverence she displayed for her gifts and for the way she quickly reached for his hand when they started walking again.

"What happened next?" she asked.

With her gone from Noelle, he hadn't been able to think clearly. He'd drifted in a daze following the searchers. "We increased our numbers with Doc Deane and Cara from his clinic, Felicity and Reverend Hammond from the saloon, and Josefina and Nacho from their restaurant. When we reached Cobb's Penn and Liam and Avis working together inside, he revealed he'd been worried when he saw Madame Bonheur striding up the street toward our end of town. He said she was carrying the snowshoes he'd traded for your curtains."

"I'm sorry I had to do that."

"I'm not."

Her eyes went wide with astonishment. "You're not?"

"The moment I heard the word snowshoes I knew where you'd be. In the deep snow off the road."

The anxiety tensing his muscles only eased when they finally stood on the road by the narrow pass. The mule he'd tied to the tree lifted its head and brayed in welcome.

Birdie's gaze darted from the beast to him. "How did a mule get here? You said you no longer went near them."

"Desperation brought us together again. I knew I'd struggle to find you in the snow, but I hoped we'd cross paths farther down the road or at the rail station. So, I fetched one of the mules from the corral behind Peregrines."

A grin curved her lips. "And galloped to my rescue."

Jack snorted. "Nothing so smooth. The ornery beast wouldn't go faster than a jolting trot. The pace gave me too much time to contemplate the fresh boot prints heading down the road. I feared they were the miners, so when they left the road I tied the mule here and followed them, and then the voices." Remembering her cry made his stomach churn.

She scanned the mule in her usual thorough way, then him as well. "You rode with only a halter and lead rope."

He shrugged. "There was no time to find a saddle. I was in a hurry." He was in a hurry again—to hold her close. He untied the mule and with the aid of a snowbank leapt onto its back. "Can I offer you a ride home?"

Her smile blinded him with happiness as she reached up to grasp his hand. He lifted her to sit side-saddle in front of him and reined the mule toward Noelle.

This time the stubborn creature moved without urging, eager to get home where it'd always been well-cared-for by Woody. He patted its neck and silently praised it for its efforts in helping him reach Birdie in time. He'd never stop thanking the mule for that gift.

"I've always wanted to ask, what's that pounding noise?" Birdie gestured in the direction of the mine.

"That's the stamp mill's steam-powered rock crusher. It makes a miner's life a tad less laborious. It's also why the mine got the nickname of *The Drum*."

On the road ahead, the distant silhouette of man strode toward them.

Birdie leaned forward eagerly. "Is that Grandpa? *Non*, Gus is thinner. This man is—" Her entire body went stiff as an oak plank as she jerked backward.

The man walked with a slight limp and whole lot of determination. Silver pistols flashed in a leather holster riding low on his hips.

"Sheriff Draven." Her brittle announcement came with a shiver that left her trembling.

He wrapped his arms around her and cradled her against his wildly beating heart. "It's time to tell him your name."

"And then?"

He wasn't sure. He was only certain about one thing. "Whatever happens, we'll face it together."

CHAPTER 21

*A*lmost four days had passed since Birdie first entered the Golden Nugget Saloon with eleven other brides and one matchmaker. Today when she walked in, she didn't scan the room. She didn't have to. She'd already found what she was looking for and more.

She held the hand of her husband-to-be and smiled up at the man she loved. Jack returned her gaze with an intensity that made her wonder if his thoughts had gone a step further—already imagining them back at Peregrines' Post and upstairs in their bedroom.

"Get ready for another wedding, folks!" Gus hollered as he shepherded them away from the crisp air that'd followed them across the threshold.

The room erupted in a round of hearty "congratulations" and the squeaking of tables and chairs being pushed aside to allow everyone to gather close for the event.

When her arm brushed something prickly, she finally wrenched her gaze away from Jack. Gus had maneuvered them to a spot by an evergreen tree decorated with three entwined hearts made from fine silver—that reminded her

of Culver's flask—and a handful of equally beautiful orna-
ments painted in contrasting colors. A partridge, two doves,
three hens and a—

Her breath caught in her throat as she reverently
touched the replica of the tiny gray bird with a white breast
and a black cap that'd sang to her in the forest when she
was all alone.

"Reminds me of you again," Jack whispered close to her
ear. "Grandpa added the same bird to your wedding
present."

She instinctively slipped her hand inside her coat to
ensure the leather case was still attached to her belt. She
smiled when her fingertips touched the engraving of the
small round bird.

"My chickadee," Jack said as he kissed her cheek. "Since
you came to town, you've become my favorite bird," his tone
turned teasing, "when you're not in flight."

She let go of Gus' gift and grabbed both of Jack's hands
so she could face him fully. "God willing, I'll never fly again.
At least not away from you. Flying toward you is something
I'm keen to do every day."

"We share the same goal, and with the help of Noelle,
Draven, and the Braverys, we'll never be parted again."

She nodded even though she still had trouble believing
what they'd learned from the sheriff.

Although glowering and impatient, the bounty hunter
turned lawman had listened to her story and when she'd
told him her real name, he'd done the unthinkable. He'd
laughed. So abruptly and briefly she questioned now if it
had really happened.

With his missing eye and scarred face, he certainly
hadn't looked any more approachable than the first day

she'd seen him. But what he'd said had toppled a heavy burden from her heart.

He'd explained that when Lachlan and Élodie Bravery had come to Noelle to deliver their findings about Jack's wife, the couple had asked Draven for a favor. Lachlan had said he'd seen a woman in Denver who he owed a debt. Fourteen years ago, he'd almost shot her and worried that event had launched the woman down a path of a life on the run.

Lachlan had requested that if Draven ever discovered Bernadette Bellamy was in trouble, Draven should contact him. This time Lachlan vowed he'd use his Winchester to defend not threaten. His wife had pledged her support as well.

Bernadette Bellamy was now under the protection of two of the most revered legends of the northwest. Not to mention two much-loved men named Peregrine.

"Stay together," the elder said while the younger replied, "Best advice you've ever given."

But when Gus grabbed his friend Ezra's arm and turned to leave, Jack protested. "Where are you going?"

"To fetch Mrs. Walters 'n anyone else we can gather from *La Maison*." Gus' gaze met hers as he paused. "Hopefully we'll find yer copper-haired friend who visited yesterday."

"Oh, it'd be wonderful if you could bring Penny."

"With a little luck, we shall. With lots more, I might even remember she's *pretty as a penny* 'n call her by her name when I see her. Hope I can locate Aggie, as well." Gus hurriedly combed his fingers through his beard and adjusted his flat cap. "She'll want to see you wed."

"Who's Aggie?" Jack asked.

Gus ducked his head and pushed Ezra toward the door.

His friend dug in his heels. "Yeah, I never heard ya mention an Aggie before."

"*Grand-père*, do you mean Agatha Boonesbury? When did you find the time to talk to her?"

"Now isn't *the time* for jawin'," Gus countered. "We need to gather as many people as possible to witness this marriage."

Ezra slapped Gus on the back. "You can't fool me, ya old geezer. You want a crowd to share your celebration."

"That I do." Gus' grin became a scowl. "I also wanna show Madwoman Bonheur that this town stands with me 'n my grandchildren. She'd better think twice before bedeviling us again."

Gus' words and new moniker for the madam made her shake then nod her head in quick order. She prayed the woman's crazy desperation to reclaim what she'd lost wouldn't lead to more threats—directed at the Peregrines or others.

She planned to use the Braverys' promise of protection to safeguard Gus and Jack as well as herself. But what of the other brides? Especially those who hadn't yet married and formed unbreakable bonds with their grooms? And who would help the poor souls who had nothing but their work under Madame Bonheur's rule?

Gus had finally got his friend moving, and they were almost at the door.

Before they left, she hastened to call out, "*Grand-père*, if you find Pearl at *La Maison*, beg her to come too, *s'il vous plaît*."

He gave her a jaunty salute before he disappeared outside.

The hullabaloo in the saloon reminded her that Gus and his friend had already rounded up quite a few witnesses and celebrators. The search party had transformed into a wedding party. Having not seen Madame Bonheur since her return, she could only assume the woman had retreated to her reduced lodgings. Birdie couldn't imagine the madam would stay hidden, or quiet, for long however.

"Hey, *chica*." Josefina tugged Birdie's sleeve impatiently. "Don't keep us waiting. Take off that coat and reveal your wedding dress."

"*Oui, montre-nous ta robe!*" Minnie's perfectly pronounced French no longer surprised Birdie. The woman had divulged some of her secrets but not all. "Show your dress," Minnie urged. "We're keen to see the divine creation a dressmaker makes for her big day."

She raised both hands in defeat. "Sadly, I have nothing worthy to reveal. I didn't have time to make a dress."

"But you're so quick with your needle." Meizhen's compliment made Birdie shake her head. Spending many years as an acrobat made Woody's wife quicker than all of the brides combined.

Jack's steadfast regard as he watched her while addressing the women made her pulse race. "You ladies should've seen how fast my wife was with her scissors when I found her in a tree an hour ago."

My wife. Her heart swelled with happiness at how easily he said the words along with the return of his teasing tone. She'd gladly have given up every inch of cloth she wore to escape her fall and land back in his arms.

Her current attire was something she'd never imagined she'd wear on her wedding day, but she didn't care. Well, not as long as no one discovered her state of undress. Luckily, her long coat concealed her well.

It did not however hide her from the frigid air that, when the saloon door banged open, gusted across the floor and up her legs. When she shivered, Jack moved to block the chill with his body.

Even though dressmaking had been her passion for as long as she could recall, Noelle kept reminding her of the importance of winter clothing. Her lips parted on a silent gasp. She'd never given Jack and Gus their Christmas scarves! The instant they got back to Peregrines, she'd present them promptly.

No more waiting.

Gus waved a trio of smiling women through the saloon door. Mrs. Walters, Penny, and Agatha raced to her side.

She hugged each of them and the other brides as well. So many had made it, but not— Unease constricted her chest as she asked, "Where's Pearl? Couldn't you find her at *La Maison?*"

Gus cocked his head as if trying to remember. "Never got there. Met Aggie 'n her flock coming this way. Liam told 'em to head to the Nugget."

Mrs. Walters' usually sharp and determined green eyes shone with the same worry that gripped Birdie. "Pearl wasn't with us. As to her location..." The matchmaker heaved a sigh. "Your guess is as good as mine."

Birdie's shoulders stiffened as she contemplated the places Pearl might be. "I hope she's all right." *I hope she's nowhere near Madame Bonheur.*

Jack's large hand enveloped hers and squeezed reassuringly. "We'll make sure she's all right. We'll do it together."

Tears blurred her vision. How far they'd come in four days. It was hard to believe she'd once refrained from saying Pearl's name for fear Jack might question her desire to give a dress to a fallen woman, or that he might not stand by a bride who had a history of thievery in her past.

Jack was the man for her. A man she was eager to marry.

She pulled him toward Reverend Hammond who waited with his Bible in his hands and his new wife, Felicity, by his side.

The man nearly blinded her with his beaming smile. "It gives me immense pleasure to see the two of you are finally ready to marry. You're doing Noelle a great service by saying your vows."

Three couples had gotten hitched. She and Jack would make the count four, but Noelle still needed eight additional marriages in order to meet the railroad's deadline in nine days. Would the town, that was about to become her home, succeed?

"Jack. Miss Bell." The reverend nodded to them in turn. "Let us proceed. Do you—?"

She shook her head. "I cannot get married unless you call me Bernadette Bellamy."

Both the reverend and Felicity stared at her in wide-eyed bafflement.

She turned in a circle as she addressed the crowd. "My real name is Bernadette Bellamy. But after the ceremony, please call me Birdie. Or Mrs. Peregrine." She stopped turning when she faced Jack. "I'm eager to leap into my new life."

"Reverend Hammond, you'd better marry us quickly." Jack bent to whisper close to her ear. "Because I want to—"

"Take me home." She used his nearness to steal a kiss. "I know what you're thinking. We have unfinished business."

"In the freight office?" The heat in his golden eyes told her he was anticipating another location.

She combed her fingers through his enticingly windswept and wild hair. "We have much to do. But I'll only assist you in your work after we finish what we started upstairs."

Jack's voice turned deep and solemn, sounding exactly as she'd imagined he would when he said his vows. "Never doubt for a moment, *mon univers*, that you truly are my everything. All of our matchmakers did their jobs perfectly when they matched us."

∿

Thank you for reading *The Calling Birds: The Fourth Day!* I hope you enjoyed Birdie and Jack and, of course, Grandpa Gus' adventures in the town of Noelle. Even though they've won their happily-ever-after, the future of Noelle remains uncertain.

Can eight more couples get married by the twelfth day of Christmas? Will the town of Noelle receive its railroad line and not only survive, but thrive beyond Christmas 1876? Will Jack's brother Max come home to Noelle?

Keep reading for a look at the next book in the *Twelve Days of Christmas Mail-Order Brides* multi-author series and also for an excerpt from *Robyn: A Christmas Bride*—Max Peregrine and Robyn Llewellyn's story that follows one year later in Christmas 1877.

The Gold Ring: The Fifth Day
The 12 days of Christmas Mail-Order Brides Series

By Caroline Lee

On the fifth day of Christmas, my true love gave to me...

Pearl knows she'll only ever be a soiled dove. Her chance to be anything more was snatched away long ago, and the bitterness has eaten at her for years. What keeps her looking to the future is the opportunity to take care of and protect the other working girls at *La Maison des Chats*... Well that, and one particular customer who holds her heart, even if he would never consider a life with someone like her.

On Christmas Eve, a dozen new brides arrive in Noelle and are forced to take up residence in La Maison. Pearl is happy to be able to offer comfort and support, because the poor things need her help...even if their very presence is a sharp reminder that she can never be one of them.

But when the Reverend's scheme to get the brides married off falls through on only the second day of Christmas, it looks like the town will never be stable enough to entice the railroad spur they all desperately need. So Pearl agrees to a deception that will not only save the town, but bring her what she desperately wants: a marriage—even a pretend one—with the man she loves.

Little do they know just how dangerous this deception will turn out to be.

~

~

THE 12 DAYS OF CHRISTMAS MAIL-ORDER BRIDES

Twelve men. Twelve brides. Twelve days to save a town.

Christmas, 1876: Noelle, Colorado is in danger of becoming a ghost town if the railroad decides to bypass the mountaintop mining community. Determined to prove their town is thriving, twelve men commit to ordering brides before the railroad's deadline six days into the New Year.

Each of the twelve women has her own reason for signing up to become a mail-order bride. But after they arrive in the uncivilized settlement, they aren't so sure they've made the right decision. Neither are the grooms.
Will the marriages happen in time to save Noelle?
The countdown starts on Christmas Day.

THE 12 BOOKS IN THE SERIES

The Partridge, The First Day - by Kit Morgan
The Dove, The Second Day - by Shanna Hatfield
The Hens, The Third Day - by Merry Farmer
The Calling Birds, The Fourth Day - by Jacqui Nelson
The Gold Ring, The Fifth Day - by Caroline Lee
The Goose, The Sixth Day - by Peggy L Henderson
The Swan, The Seventh Day - by Piper Huguley
The Maid, The Eighth Day - by Rachel Wesson
The Dancing Lady, The Ninth Day - by Mimi Milan
The Lord, The Tenth Day - by Danica Favorite
The Piper, The Eleventh Day - by Amanda McIntyre
The Drum, The Twelfth Day - by E.E. Burke

DEAR READER

I hope you enjoyed *The Calling Birds* and Jack and Birdie's quest to find love, peace, and a forever home in the town of Noelle.

If you did, please consider writing a review or say hello via the usual places including email. Every single review helps. No matter how long or short, they are a heartfelt gift that is sincerely appreciated.

Hearing from readers makes my day and keeps me motivated to write my next book. Looking forward to hearing from you!

Review on AMAZON
www.amazon.com/author/jacquinelson
www.amazon.com/dp/B077R6BK7R

Review on GOODREADS
www.goodreads.com/jacquinelson

Review on BOOKBUB
www.bookbub.com/authors/jacqui-nelson

STORY INSPIRATION & NOTES

When asked, which day of Christmas would you like to write? I immediately chose *The Fourth Day* because with the title *The Calling Birds,* I could use the name Jack Peregrine. His name was inspired by Inspector Jack Robinson from the *Miss Fisher's Murder Mysteries* novels & TV series and the *Miss Peregrine's Home for Peculiar Children* novel & movie. Jack and then Birdie's names came to me lightning quick, and might not have worked as well in more specifically titled 12 days stories such as the Hens, Doves, Geese, or Swans.

So, I chose the more generic title and then, as seems to be my nature, I became really specific. *Peregrines' Post and Freight* had to be the plural because it's a family-run business. The word "post" had to come before "freight" because when shortened to *Peregrines' Post,* it stood for not only a postal office but a post on which a bird might rest AND a place to make a final stand - while trying to keep a business alive and a family together.

Next, I decided I needed four birds to form my family because it's *The Fourth Day,* after all. Jack's brother, Max, and Grandpa Gus came to life. Now I cannot imagine *The Calling Birds* without Gus. Jack and Gus' banter was inspired by my relationship with my mom. She was great fun but also incredibly stubborn (to the point where I'd worry for her safety). It became our running joke where I'd call her determined, but I meant stubborn - and she knew it. She was never absentminded, though. That feature is mine but, like Gus, I'd rather find ways to get around my shortcomings instead of dwelling on them.

~ Jacqui

ACKNOWLEDGMENTS

Thank you to my editors Nora and Liette for making my story sparkle. Thank you to Quinn and Liette for making my French sing. Thank you to Marjorie and Marion Ann for our many talks about life and writing. Thank you to my advance reader team, *Jacqui's Posse of Book Angels*, for loving my books and saying so.

Thank you to the other authors in *The Twelve Days of Christmas Mail-Order Brides* series for making the creation of the town of Noelle—and the twelve happily-ever-afters that happen there during Christmas 1876—so much fun.

ROBYN: A CHRISTMAS BRIDE

The sequel to *The Calling Birds*.
Read what happens one year later in Noelle 1877…

∿

Who's the perfect match for a flame-haired Welsh tomboy who loves driving wagons?

Raised by three free-spirited older brothers, Robyn Llewellyn has learned to fight for what she wants—and now she wants to transform her boss and best friend, Max Peregrine, into a lifelong partner. Determined to become the image of what a marriage-minded man wants, Robyn trades her trousers for a dress and heads to Max's hometown of Noelle, Colorado. But changing who she is with the help of the now happily married Brides of Noelle puts her friendship with Max at risk.

Who's the perfect match for a work-addicted Denver business owner who loves his independence?

Defying his brother and grandpa's wishes for him to stay with them in Noelle, Max Peregrine has created his dream job—leading a highly successful branch of Peregrines' Post and Freight while working beside Robyn, the only person who makes him smile every day. But when she leaves without a word, Max follows her to Noelle where the choices they both must face could make it impossible for them to stay together beyond Christmas Day.

Inspired by *My Fair Lady, The Gift of the Magi,* and the spirit of gift giving, *Robyn: A Christmas Bride* is a classic Western historical love story set in a small town high in the mountains during Christmas 1877.

∿

EXCERPT ~ CHAPTER 1

Denver, Colorado
December 21, 1877

"She's gone?" Max Peregrine shouted, disbelief then panic raising his voice to a roar. "Where?"

Lined up shoulder to shoulder inside the Denver office of Peregrines' Post and Freight, the three Llewellyn brothers studied him intently, not with surprise but curiosity. And something more. Something his careening thoughts couldn't identify.

Brynmor, the eldest by several years, heaved a sympathetic sounding sigh. "She's—"

"Fine," Heddwyn interrupted, embracing his status as the swift-talking middle brother who needed to do everything quick, including driving freight wagons at breakneck speed. He shot his brothers a secretive glance. "Remember our plan. He sounds upset, but we need to know more."

"Stuff your plans!" Max threw down his pencil and stormed around the desk where he'd been working on his ledgers. He'd throttle his answers from Robyn's brothers if need be. "Why—did—she—leave!?"

Griffin, the youngest but also the largest, folded his arms over his barrel of a chest. "He sounds more than upset."

"Good." Standing on either side of their flame-haired baby brother, Brynmor and Heddwyn spoke and nodded in unison, like matching musclebound bookends with the same auburn hair and sky-blue eyes. Except Bryn had one eye clouded white. Max had yet to learn why.

The Llewellyns were fond of talk but notoriously unforthcoming on certain subjects. Like, at the moment, Robyn's departure.

"He's regretting something," Griffin added.

Max froze. Leave it to Griff to pinpoint Max's state of mind while never addressing his own. Griff's hair color matched his sister's, but his reputation as the Llewellyn sibling with a short fuse was his alone.

"I regret"—he unlocked his clenched jaw and tried to speak normally—"that your sister might have put herself in jeopardy."

Heddwyn snorted. "Little Red can take care of herself."

"Hedd's right. The wee one is all grown-up," Bryn proclaimed with another sigh.

"She's as tough as she is beautiful." Griff's gaze narrowed, studying him even more keenly. "Or do you believe otherwise?"

"I don't," Max muttered, thinking of Robyn's lean strength, steely blue gaze, and stunning smile. A smile he'd been blessed to see every day since he moved to Denver. A smile he craved more than a miner coveted gold. A smile that had become increasingly melancholy of late. "Whatever's wrong and wherever she's gone, she needn't be alone. I would've traveled with her."

"You sure 'bout that?" Hedd released a low whistle as he pointed at Max's face. "Look! Dog Bone's turning the same shade of red as Ruddy does when he's near to exploding."

In Welsh, *Griff* meant *ruddy,* but that hothead remained poker-faced as he said, "We have eyes, Peaceful. No need telling us something we can plainly see."

Max's entire body burned with outrage. Not because of the teasing titles the Llewellyns loved to dole out, for themselves and others. In Welsh, *Heddwyn* meant *blessed peace*, a constant source of ribbing for a man who had too much energy to stand still. Max had learned to look below the surface of their name tomfoolery after Robyn revealed her brothers called him Dog Bone because he never stopped gnawing problems into submission.

He didn't give up. A trait all of the Llewellyns found admirable. If they assigned you a name, even one you didn't find flattering, it meant you'd earned their respect. They didn't waste their time on people they didn't like.

Robyn's explanation along with her easy smile had ended his dislike for long conversations. But only with her. They'd talked about everything after that, argued as much as they'd agreed, but always ended up smiling.

No topic had been taboo, or so he thought. Why hadn't she spoken to him before she left? And how could her brothers question his resolve, especially when it came to Robyn?

Their lack of faith left him not only furious but frustrated and flummoxed. "If your sister asked, I'd have gone *anywhere* with her."

Bryn raised an eyebrow in challenge. "You said differently in the past."

"I did not."

"Did too," Hedd shot back. "Then Rob said she had to go there. No other place would do."

"Took the Clydesdale." Griff thrust his thumb over his shoulder. "In better weather, she'd be there by now."

Max's gaze leapt in the direction he'd indicated, hoping to see Robyn behind her brothers. That this was all some colossal joke.

Driven by a fickle wind, his world spun faster than the snow outside the window. She couldn't be gone. Not in such a storm. Not when he needed her, when they all needed her. She was the thread that held everything together. Did her brothers seriously believe he wouldn't have accompanied her on any journey? They'd lost their minds. He couldn't do the same. He had to find Robyn.

~

To read more about *Robyn: A Christmas Bride*, visit
JacquiNelson.com

RESCUING RAVEN
Deadwood 1876...

In a gold rush storm, can an unlikely pair rescue each other?
Raven wants to save one person. Charlie wants to save the
world. Their warring nations thrust them together but duty
pulled them apart—until their paths crossed again in
Deadwood for a fight for love.

EXCERPT ~ CHAPTER 1
August 1876, Dakota Territory

Fighting a growing impatience fueled by rage, Charlie
Jennings drew his revolver and urged his horse through the
trees flanking the Deadwood Trail. Below him, an
Appaloosa with the strikingly similar color of his own horse
—white covered from head to hock in chestnut spots—was
rein-tied to the back of a buckboard. If the horse hadn't
caught his attention, he might not have given the transport a
second look.

He might not have seen her.

The wagon rattled forward carrying one silent and seven
grumbling passengers. When a bend in the trail cast the sun
in the eyes of the guards, one riding behind and the other in
front, he charged his spotted mare down onto the road.

Everyone in the wagon, except for the cowering raven-
haired woman, screamed. The driver jerked on the reins.

The horses skidded to a halt. The guards scrambled for their weapons.

The click of his revolver being cocked made them all freeze.

The silence that followed was as heated as the summer sun on his back. The guards glared at him through squinted eyes. He kept his focus on them as well—lined up in a neat row down the barrel of his Colt Peacemaker.

"Jennings," growled the closest man, who went by the name Big Bill. "You shouldn't be here."

"Yeah," hollered Bill's partner, a stranger who resembled a beanpole.

Frontier trails and towns had a way of attracting similarly named men, including the Charlies like him. They also had a fondness for embellishment. The deck was stacked in favor of the rear guard being called Skinny Sam or Loudmouth Pete.

"We heard you were guidin' a miner 'n his four kids, the ones who lost their ma, away from Deadwood." At least Skinny hadn't heard, and used, the double-barreled moniker Charlie had been saddled with since arriving in the Black Hills.

"But you," he shot back, "didn't hear that my job finished ahead of schedule."

"Well," Bill said on a long breath, "ain't that a spot of bad luck."

"Not for one of your passengers." He didn't look her way. He'd already seen enough: a ragtag assortment of women, one hunched with her dark head over her wrists tied to the wagon.

To read the rest of *Rescuing Raven*, visit my website
JacquiNelson.com and sign up for my newsletter.

～

GAMBLING HEART SERIES

Between Love & Lies - Book 1

Between Home & Heartbreak - Book 2

～

STEAM! ROMANCE AND RAILS SERIES

Adella's Enemy

ABOUT THE AUTHOR

Fall in love with a new Old West... where the men are steadfast and the women are adventurous. You'll find Wild West scouts, spies, cardsharps, wilderness guides, and trick-riding superstars in my stories. Those are my heroines. Wait till you meet my heroes! My love for historical romance adventures with grit and passion came from watching Western movies while growing up on a cattle farm in northern Canada. I've been nominated for over 20 awards and won the RWA® Golden Heart® & the Laramie® — but my best reward is hearing from readers who have enjoyed my stories.

Join me on...

JacquiNelson.com
www.amazon.com/author/jacquinelson
www.goodreads.com/jacquinelson
www.bookbub.com/authors/jacqui-nelson
www.facebook.com/JacquiNelsonAuthor
www.facebook.com/JacquiNelsonBooks
www.twitter.com/Jacqui_Nelson

Email me at...
Jacqui@JacquiNelson.com

For updates on my new releases, giveaways and events, subscribe to my newsletter on my website JacquiNelson.com

Made in the USA
Coppell, TX
24 November 2021

66386813R00098